Save the Ponies!

GILLIAN BAXTER

Angela and Ian are very upset when Uncle Arthur has to find new stabling for his pantomime ponies, Magic and Moonshine. Luckily the local brewery offers them temporary shelter, among the giant Shire horses. But the situation is not resolved until the ponies themselves provide the ideal answer to the problem.

GILLIAN BAXTER

Save the Ponies!

Illustrated by Elisabeth Grant

A Magnet Book

Also by Gillian Baxter in Magnet Books

PONIES BY THE SEA
SPECIAL DELIVERY
PANTOMIME PONIES
PONIES IN HARNESS

First published in Great Britain 1971
by Methuen Children's Books Ltd
Paperback edition first published 1976
by Methuen Children's Books Ltd
Magnet edition first published 1982
by Methuen Children's Books Ltd
11 New Fetter Lane, London EC4P 4EE
Text copyright © 1971 Gillian Baxter
Illustrations copyright © 1971
Methuen Children's Books Ltd
Cover photograph © 1982 Methuen Children's Books Ltd

Printed and bound in Great Britain by
Cox & Wyman Ltd, Reading

ISBN 0 416 57160 3

Contents

1 · The Letter   *page*   7
2 · Horseman's Sunday   25
3 · Among the giants   42
4 · Settling in   60
5 · More like man's work   78
6 · Horse power   94
7 · Not a joke any more   110
8 · The new landlord   125

1 · The letter

The sound of briskly trotting hooves in the quiet, drab London street made several people look round. Some children looked up from their game on the steps outside number ten, and two ladies with shopping baskets paused in their talk to stare. Someone glanced out of a lace-curtained ground floor window, and stayed there a moment, gazing out, and the milkman looked up from stacking crates on to his electric milk float.

The two tiny, cream-coloured ponies were in perfect step, their necks arched, their little ears pricked, and their creamy manes and tails floating. Against their pale coats the black, patent leather harness shone, and behind them the miniature landau carriage ran smoothly on its rubber-rimmed wheels.

On the driving seat sat a fair-haired girl of about eight. She held the reins lightly and carefully in her hands, and her face was intent. Her long hair, tied back with a blue ribbon, was blown by the breeze as they moved along. Beside her sat a tall, thin, red-faced man with thin grey hair and thick bushy eyebrows. He, too, was intent on the ponies, and the way that the girl was driving.

Only the boy sitting in the lower, central part of the carriage behind them was less intent on the ponies. He was looking out instead at the passing terraces of rather sooty houses, the small shops, and the parked cars. To tell the truth, Ian was slightly bored. He was fond of Magic and Moonshine, the two little pantomime ponies who pulled Cinderella's coach on the stage each year, and who did their own routine of tricks as well, and usually he quite enjoyed going out with them in the carriage. Today, though, he felt slightly left out. He had felt like that quite a lot lately, now that Uncle Arthur was married to Grace, and she had taken the place of their mother, who had died with their father such a long time ago.

Until they had come to live with Uncle

Arthur, Angela and Ian had moved about, living with different relatives, and it had been to Ian that Angela had turned for help or support. He had felt responsible for her, and the two of them had needed one another. Now, Angela turned to Grace more than to Ian when she wanted

help, and sometimes he felt rather on the outside of things. And it was Angela who had learned to drive the ponies most quickly, and who handled them the best.

'Steady now,' Uncle Arthur was saying, as they approached the end of the street. 'Back to a walk in good time, remember, and halt at the

9

corner. Never let them go up to a corner fast, there might be something coming.'

Angela tightened the reins, making sure to keep a steady, even pull on both reins, and the two tiny ponies bent their heads to their bits and slowed up. Uncle Arthur's hands were hovering over Angela's, just in case, but he did not have to touch them. Angela's hands, and her firm 'whoa' brought the whole outfit to a smooth halt in just the right place.

'Hop out, Ian, and make sure it's clear to cross,' ordered Uncle Arthur, and Ian got out over the low door and went forward into the next quiet road to make sure that nothing was coming. With two ponies harnessed together extra time was needed to make a turn, and it was best to be quite sure that it was safe.

There was nothing coming. Ian signalled to Uncle Arthur, and he said, 'Right. Remember now, Angie, don't let them come round too fast.'

The ponies moved forward, at a walk now, Angela increased her feel on the 'off', or right-hand rein, telling Magic, who was on the out-side, to start turning. At the same time she kept a firm feel on the 'near' side, or left rein, preventing Moonshine from turning too fast and barging into his partner. The inside reins from both ponies' bits were fastened to those of their partners, and holding one pony back also helped to check the other.

As the little carriage with its miniature team came round Ian hopped back into his seat behind Angela and Uncle Arthur. He was trying not to remember the mess that he had once made of turning Magic and Moonshine. He had been in a hurry, hearing a car coming in the distance, and he had completely forgotten the need to steady Moonshine as well as pulling Magic's rein to bring him round. The ponies had started to turn much too sharply, scrambling round with the carriage skidding sideways behind them, and Uncle Arthur had had to take the reins from him quickly to prevent an accident.

'Everyone can make mistakes,' Uncle Arthur had told him afterwards, but Ian had always felt humiliated by the incident.

The road into which they had turned led them through a square, past one of the overgrown, leafy gardens of which there were several in the district. As the ponies trotted past, the sound of their hooves echoing slightly from the tall, shabby houses, Ian noticed that the leaves on the tall plane trees were just beginning to turn gold. The summer was almost over. School would be starting again soon, and for the ponies the busy season of stage shows and pantomimes would be beginning again. In two weeks Uncle Arthur was planning to take the ponies and their carriage to Horseman's Sunday, on Epsom Downs, when a special service was held for horses, and the day after that the autumn term began.

Ian knew that he was looking forward to school again, although he did get teased a bit about the ponies. That was different for Angela, too. The girls of her own age all envied and admired her for having an uncle who owned pantomime ponies, and she was popular because of them. That, too, had given her extra confidence to stand on her own feet more and need Ian's support less.

They were nearly home now. Ian jumped out again to conduct them across another road, and they were turning into their own street. This was a long street of terraced houses and a few small shops, with a public house at the end.

Even in the bright summer sunlight it was rather dark, over-shadowed by the tall office blocks behind it. Ian and Angela had thought at first that it was a dreary sort of street, but now it was home to them and they no longer noticed.

The ponies began to slow down as they approached the short row of shops where they lived. Uncle Arthur had the paper shop, and a board above the door read 'A. Perry. Newsagent, Tobacconist, and Confectioner.' It was the first shop in the row. Racks outside the door held copies of local and evening newspapers, and the windows were attractively arranged with displays of sweets and cigarettes, magazines, and plastic toys. Grace did the window displays now, sometimes with Angela to help her. They had taken the job over from Uncle Arthur, who had never enjoyed it much.

Outside the shop Angela brought the ponies to a halt, and Uncle Arthur stepped down from the seat and came round to the off side to take the reins from her. He was stepping back up when Grace opened the shop door. She was a nice-looking, dark-haired woman, quite a bit younger than Uncle Arthur.

'Hello,' she said. 'I'll put the kettle on, and open up the gate for you.'

'Thanks, Grace. We're coming right round,' Uncle Arthur told her.

He drove the ponies on to the end of the shops, and the corner of the road where the pub stood. Round here, on the left, was the entrance to the cinder path which ran between the back yards of the two rows of houses, Uncle Arthur's row and the one behind.

It was a tight and ticklish job, turning the pair and their carriage into the narrow pathway, which was little more than the width of an ordinary car. Uncle Arthur, though, brought the ponies round with a practised touch on the reins, judging his distances exactly, and the ponies' hooves and the light wheels crunched on to the cinders. Magic snorted and the sound echoed back from the high fences and walls on either side. Grace had their own back gate open, and she went to the ponies' heads as they stopped outside. Uncle Arthur, Angela, and Ian got down, and Ian began to help Uncle Arthur to unhitch the ponies.

'Were they good?' asked Grace, rubbing Moonshine's nose as he breathed softly over her wrists. 'How did your driving go, Angela?'

'They were very good,' Angela told her. 'And it was lovely. I hardly needed any help with them, did I, Uncle Arthur?'

'No, you did very well, very well indeed,' replied Uncle Arthur.

'How about you, Ian?' asked Grace. 'Enjoy the ride?'

'Oh, it was all right,' muttered Ian, who was bending over one of Moonshine's traces. Grace looked at him hard, but he did not look round, and she said no more. Then he and Angela led the ponies through the gate into the little yard and Uncle Arthur followed them pulling the light little carriage.

A long shed with a slanting roof was built against the wall at the path end of the yard, and this was where Magic and Moonshine lived. Inside it was divided into two by poles and wooden partitions, and a narrow gangway ran between the two halves, with hay stored at the far end of it. Grace had put feeds ready in both ponies' mangers, and after they had both had a drink they plunged their noses into the mixture of pony cubes, bran, and a scattering of oats. They did not have too many oats, or they would have become fresh and naughty.

Uncle Arthur pushed the carriage into its place between the shed and the wall which divided the yard from that of their neighbour, and then he came in to make sure that all was well in the stable. He was followed in by Partner, the large ginger cat, who was a great friend of the ponies.

'Not sweating, are they?' asked Uncle Arthur running a hand down Magic's shoulder. Although he never actually admitted it, Ian and Angela suspected that Magic was Uncle Arthur's favourite of the two ponies. He was the quickest and cleverest, and also the cheekiest of the pair.

'No, they dried off before we got home, and they haven't started again,' replied Angela. 'They feel quite dry now.'

'Good,' said Uncle Arthur. 'That's the way. You know Grace, that carriage really was a good buy. It makes a fine advertisement for them. We might even get some bookings with it now that they've really settled to the job.'

'And of course it did make a wonderful wedding coach,' added Grace, laughing, and Angela remembered coming home from Grace and

16

Uncle Arthur's wedding. Uncle Arthur had been driving, with Grace inside the little carriage in her lovely dress, and herself and Ian perched on the step at the back. That was nearly six months ago now, before the ponies went away for their summer rest at grass, and before she and Ian had started to learn to drive. It seemed ages ago. Angela felt as though they had lived with Grace and Uncle Arthur always.

While they were talking and tidying up the stable Partner had paused for a moment in the doorway with one front paw raised and his whiskers pushed forward. Now he jumped up on to the partition on Magic's side of the stable. He stood there for a second, and then leaped lightly on to the pony's back. Magic glanced round at him, still chewing, with his ears pricked and bran dust clinging to his whiskers, and then he turned back to his feed. Partner turned round once and then lay down in the warm, broad hollow over the pony's loins and began to wash his face.

'Come on,' said Grace. 'Watching them eat is making me hungry. Let's get our own tea.'

The back door, at the top of a short flight of

stone steps, took them into the kitchen, bright
and shining since Grace had taken over. The
children washed their hands at the spotless sink,
sniffing the appetizing smell of newly-baked
cakes, and then went through to the living room,
the only other downstairs room besides the
shop.

Uncle Arthur's living-room was rather
crowded. Chairs, tables, a shabby settee, a giant
sideboard, an upright piano, and tall sets of
crowded book shelves took up nearly all the
space. The walls between the furniture were
almost covered by Uncle Arthur's collection of
old playbills, and his photographs of the stars of
silent films. It was tidier than it had once been,
however, for Grace saw to it that there was not
too much clutter on the shelves and on top of
the cupboard and the piano. The only things
now on top of the piano were several framed
photographs, one of Grace and Uncle Arthur
after their wedding, one of the ponies on stage
in a pantomime, and one of Angela and Ian on
a day out by the sea. There was also a flourishing cactus garden in a green plastic trough.
Over it all hung the cage where Bluey, the
blue budgerigar, chattered to them, out of

reach of tempting Partner into thoughts of catching him.

In the middle of the room the table was laid for tea, and the children's eyes went at once to the results of Grace's baking. There were scones and fairy cakes, a sponge cake with chocolate butter icing, and some sausage rolls. There was also a salad with hard-boiled eggs in it, plenty of bread and butter, a jar of Grace's home-made jam, and the cheese dish. Uncle Arthur rubbed his hands together in appreciation.

'My goodness, Grace, that looks good,' he said. 'You must have been working all after-noon.'

'Not really.' Grace put the tea-pot down on its mat, and sat down herself. 'I made the pastry before June came for her piano lesson and the scones are from yesterday, hotted up. I just had the sponges to make when June had gone. I had plenty of time, with its being early closing day, and I felt like doing some cooking.'

'And we're all jolly glad you did.' Uncle Arthur picked up the plate of bread and butter. 'Now, who wants what?'

They had reached the cake stage when Grace suddenly said, 'Oh, Arthur, there was a letter for you in the afternoon post. I'd forgotten all about it. It's behind the clock.'

'Was there?' Uncle Arthur got up, his mouth still full of cake. 'Better see what it is I suppose.'

He picked up the letter and came back to the table, passing his cup to Grace for more tea before he tore open the envelope. Angela went on asking Grace questions about making butter icing, and only Ian noticed that Uncle Arthur's face had gone pale, and that his cake was lying forgotten on his plate. The hand which was holding the letter began to shake slightly, and then Uncle Arthur said, 'Oh, my goodness. Oh dear.'

'What is it?' Grace looked up sharply. 'Is something wrong, Arthur?'

'It's this letter. It's from George Manners, old Fred Manners' son.' Uncle Arthur stared at her down the table. 'He's our landlord now, since old Fred died in July. He says the ponies have got to go. He says having them in the yard spoils the tone of the row and, as he's putting his property up for sale, he doesn't want the price kept down by the presence of backyard livestock.'

'But can he do that?' asked Grace. 'Didn't

you have an agreement about them with Fred Manners?'

'Yes, I did. But only with old Fred. It was a gentleman's agreement really, nothing in writing.' Uncle Arthur's eyes went back to the letter. 'Oh dear, oh dear. And when we get a new landlord he isn't likely to want them back either. My goodness, what ever can we do?'

'I'm sure we'll think of something,' said Grace encouragingly. 'They aren't doing any harm out there. No-one round here objects to them, so surely we can persuade young Mr Manners to change his mind?'

'I doubt it, I really do.' Uncle Arthur was

staring down at the letter. 'He's very much a business man, this George, quite different from his father. If he's decided that he'll get a better price with them out of the way, then he won't change.'

'Has he given any date for having them out?' asked Grace.

'Yes, yes, he has.' Uncle Arthur looked up. 'He's given me three weeks to find them a new stable.'

'Well, that's quite a long time,' Grace pointed out. 'We'll find somewhere before then.'

'I don't know.' Uncle Arthur shook his head. He had forgotten all about his tea. 'Most of the old stables round here are garages now.'

'Oh Uncle Arthur, there must be somewhere,' Angela's eyes were wide and anxious. 'They're only little, they don't need much room.'

'They need a proper stable, just the same.' Uncle Arthur had handed the letter to Grace to read. 'Oh dear, just when everything was going so well. I really don't know what to do.'

The letter had spoiled the end of tea completely. No-one felt like eating any more cake or drinking more tea when soon Magic and

Moonshine might be without a home. Grace stood up and began stacking plates together, and Uncle Arthur went out to the yard and the ponies. No-one followed him. Angela and Ian helped Grace to clear away, and then found tea-cloths to start drying up.

'What do you think Uncle Arthur will do?' Angela asked quietly, a few minutes later.

'Oh, he'll find somewhere, I'm sure,' Grace told her cheerfully. 'There's no need to worry.'

'I thought the shop belonged to Uncle Arthur?' said Ian, drying a jug.

'No, he pays rent for it, but he has a long lease,' explained Grace. 'That's an agreement that he can stay here for a long time. But of course it doesn't apply to the ponies, only to people, although the old landlord didn't mind him keeping them here. He owned all this row from here to "The Red Lion" and the wine shop on the corner.'

When Uncle Arthur came indoors again he was a little more cheerful. He said that he had thought of several places he could try for stabling, although it wouldn't be the same as having the ponies in the yard. But the atmosphere was happier by Angela and Ian's bedtime, and they even finished up the evening with a lively game of 'Happy Families'. Tomorrow, Uncle Arthur said, he would start asking round about new stabling.

2 · Horseman's Sunday

For the next two weeks Uncle Arthur searched
the district steadily for new stabling for Magic
and Moonshine. Gradually, as more and more
people said that they could not help, his cheer-
fulness began to vanish again. All the possible
places seemed to be already in use, for storage,
or as garages, and although almost everyone
said that they would like to be able to help,
none of them actually could. By the weekend of Horseman's Sunday, just before Angela
and Ian went back to school, even Grace's
attempts to cheer him up were beginning to
fail.

'I'm not sure that we ought to go,' said Uncle
Arthur, at breakfast time on Sunday. 'There's a
fellow I could see over at Balham, he used to
keep a pony for his fruit barrow, but it's a long

way out, and he's probably got a van in the stable now.'

'I think we should go,' said Grace. 'After all, you might just as easily meet someone who can help us on the downs. And you said you'd never missed a Horseman's Sunday since you got the ponies. It would be a shame to miss one now.'

'All right.' Uncle Arthur gave in, much to Angela's relief. In spite of the doubt about the ponies' future she had still been looking forward to Horseman's Sunday.

Having made the decision to go, Uncle Arthur cheered up once more.

'Come along then,' he instructed the children. 'It could be their last public appearance, but let's make it a good one. All hands to the grooming, now, while Grace gets on with packing the lunch.'

The carriage, which was kept covered by a tarpaulin, had been washed down and polished the day before, for deep down Uncle Arthur had always intended to keep to the plan to go. It was only that at the last minute he had felt guilty about losing even a few hours of time that might have been spent stable-hunting. As well as helping to clean the carriage the children had helped to clean and polish the black, patent leather harness and to burnish the brasses which hung from it. They had worked on it in the kitchen, with thick newspapers spread around to protect Grace's clean floor, and they were both proud of their share in achieving the shining result. He hadn't felt left out then, Ian realized, while they all worked on the same absorbing task. All that remained this morning was to get the ponies themselves ready.

Magic and Moonshine knew that today something special was happening. Uncle Arthur had been out early to feed them, and now they greeted him and the children with eager wuffling sounds as they entered the shed.

'We'll have them out in the yard for grooming,' said Uncle Arthur. 'It's a fine day, and we can see better outside.'

Out in the yard Uncle Arthur started work on Magic, who was the smallest of the pair by five centimetres, but who sometimes needed a firm hand. He began by rubbing hard at the pony's cream coat with a soft body brush, scraping the grease and loose hairs out of it every now and then on the metal curry comb. Ian did the same with Moonshine, while Angela fetched a bucket half-filled with soapy water and started to scrub the ponies' small neat hooves. At present they wore iron shoes, but later, when the pantomime season began, they would wear rubber shoes instead to prevent them from slipping on the wooden boards of the stage. Or they would if they were still here, Angela remembered unhappily, as she scrubbed Magic's feet with the small brush.

Uncle Arthur had washed both ponies' tails in soapy water the day before, and now he brushed the long hair out into soft cream-coloured fans. Then he began to plait Magic's mane, weaving lengths of blue and red braid in with the hair as he worked. Angela had finished their hooves, and now she held Grace's small mending box for him, handing him needle and thread as he needed it to fasten each small neat plait.

When both ponies were groomed and plaited, and their manes and tails threaded with the coloured braid, Uncle Arthur went to fetch the van while Ian and Angela stuffed hay into two hay nets ready for the ponies to eat on the journey. Then Grace called them in to wash and put on tidy clothes, and by the time they were ready

Uncle Arthur had loaded both ponies into the van.

Uncle Arthur's van was really rather spectacular. It was a tall, rather narrow-looking vehicle with a ramp at the back for the ponies to walk up. It was brightly painted, with red mudguards and wings, green bodywork, and yellow doors. Along both sides yellow letters were painted and read 'Magic and Moonshine.' Underneath, in smaller letters, was painted 'Wonder ponies of stage and screen.' Uncle Arthur thought that it was fair enough to say 'screen' as well, because the ponies had once taken part in a television commercial, advertising shampoo.

Inside the van there was a padded partition, dividing the interior into two halves, one for each pony. They looked very comfortable and at home in there, as Uncle Arthur raised the ramp up into position behind them. The carriage had its own little trailer, which Uncle Arthur now hitched on behind.

It was rather a squash for them all in the cab, but they packed in somehow. Angela sat on Grace's knee, and there was just room for Ian between her and Uncle Arthur. The big basket of food had gone in the back, along with the hay nets, the harness, and the sack containing the ponies' own lunches of pony cubes.

It was about an hour's drive to Epsom Downs. The van and trailer could only travel quite slowly, and Uncle Arthur always drove extra carefully when he had the ponies behind him.

When they got there the wide expanse of the downs was already crowded, with horses and ponies everywhere. Horse boxes, cattle trucks, and trailers mingled with hundreds of ordinary cars in the big chalky car parks and inside the oval made by the long sweep of the white-railed racecourse. Beyond the course the wide slope of short grass and scrubby bushes was black with horses and people. Away to their right, as Uncle Arthur parked the van, the children could see the great ugly bulk of the Grandstand, from which thousands of people each year watched the racehorses in the Derby and the Oaks flash past to the finish.

'They have the service over there, beyond this side of the racecourse,' explained Uncle Arthur, pointing towards the massed crowd of horses gathering beyond the road which ran alongside the racecourse straight. 'See the loud-speakers in the middle of that clear space? Afterwards all the horses and riders and the vehicles parade round the road inside the course, and every horse and pony gets a rosette. It's quite a sight, there were nearly a thousand horses here last year.'

'It's the biggest gathering of horses and ponies in the country, isn't it?' asked Grace.

'Yes. And they don't come to try to win prizes, or anything like that. They just come for the fun of it, and to have their horses blessed,' replied Uncle Arthur.

'Is there really a service, like in Church?' asked Angela.

'Oh, yes. A short one, of course, or the horses would never stand quietly, but it is a real service,' Uncle Arthur assured her. 'There are prayers, and a reading from the Bible, a sermon, and a blessing for all the horses and ponies and the people with them.'

The service was to start at twelve o'clock, and as it was now eleven-thirty they all got down from the cab, and Uncle Arthur unhitched the trailer and lowered the van ramp to the sound of Magic's usual whinny.

Quite a lot of people gathered to watch as Ian and Uncle Arthur led the ponies out and started to harness them. Angela felt rather shy, but Magic and Moonshine, of course, were used to an audience. Magic began to 'ask' by waving one front foot in the air.

'Can I give him a lump of sugar?' a little girl asked Uncle Arthur.

'Well, just one, then, before I put his bridle on,' agreed Uncle Arthur.

Magic and Moonshine both received sugar lumps, and Uncle Arthur made them both go down on one knee to bow 'Thank you.' Then the bridles were put on, and the ponies were harnessed to the carriage. Uncle Arthur climbed on to the driving seat to take the reins, and Grace got in behind him. Ian and Angela perched on the step at the back, as they had done for the wedding. Then Uncle Arthur touched the ponies' backs lightly with the tip of the driving whip, and they were moving off, out of the car park and on to the road.

There was a policeman on duty at the crossing, where all the horses and ponies were converging to cross the road and the racecourse beyond. Uncle Arthur brought both ponies to a halt to wait for him to hold up the traffic again.

'Oh Ian, look,' gasped Angela, and Ian looked up the road towards a great oncoming rattle and clatter. A great, gleaming dark-green dray drawn by four huge, magnificent black horses was coming towards them at a slow, jangling jog. Long 'feathers' of black and white hair hung like silk from the horses' legs, and their long manes and tails were braided and plaited with coloured ribbons, far more intricately done than were Magic and Moonshine's. Gleaming brasses hung from their polished harness, and they arched their huge necks and chewed their shining bits, tossing white specks of foam on to the road. Their driver and the groom beside him wore dark-green uniforms, and there was the name of a big brewery painted along the sides of the dray in gold paint.

As they came closer the big horses made tiny Magic and Moonshine look like toys, but Magic arched his own neck harder, and whinnied a cheeky greeting.

'What are they?' Ian called to Uncle Arthur, as the dray began to turn left across the road in front of them.

'Shire horses,' Uncle Arthur called back.

'Their ancestors were the horses that knights of old rode into battle. Those four probably weigh a ton each, and they can easily pull their own weight. I know that chap driving; I meet him around the shows sometimes when the lads are giving one of their displays.'

The policeman was waving them on now, and the two tiny ponies crossed the road and went over the racecourse, crossing on to the inner road behind the towering dray.

The open, roped-off space from which the service would be conducted was by now surrounded by a mass of horses and people on foot. All the horse-drawn vehicles were on one side, and Magic and Moonshine were waved into position by a steward. They found themselves between the huge Shires with their dray and a coster-cart drawn by a fat skewbald coster pony whose driver wore the costume of a pearly king.

Once they had stopped Angela and Ian had time to gaze round at the massed ranks of horses and ponies. They were nearly all very smart, their coats polished and their tack gleaming. The riders were neatly dressed, with well-brushed coats and shining boots or shoes, and many had a flower in their button-hole. Among them, looking just as smart and fit as the horses, were a number of donkeys, grey, chocolate brown, and skewbald, one or two with foals beside them. The driver of the big Shires beamed down at Magic and Moonshine, and Uncle Arthur raised his whip in greeting.

'Hello,' called the Shires' driver. 'Those shrimps of yours look well, Arthur.'

'Bit small, beside yours,' Uncle Arthur called back.

'Booked up for the season yet?' asked the driver.

'Not yet,' replied Uncle Arthur. 'Going to be a bit tricky this year, anyway. I'm losing my stabling.'

'Got anywhere else?' asked the driver.

'Not yet. I've been trying, but without any luck,' replied Uncle Arthur. 'I've got another week to go, but I've looked just about everywhere.'

'As bad as that?' asked the driver sympathetically, and Uncle Arthur said that it was. Then their attention was drawn back to the present as a big black car slid slowly down over the grass to stop at the edge of the open space, and the Rector of a nearby village got out and stepped forward to start the service.

The short service began with a welcome from the Rector, and a prayer. Then a well-known member of the British Horse Society read the lesson from the Book of Job, the verse about the war-horse, which made Ian think of pictures he had seen of snorting Arabian chargers.

After the lesson the Rector talked for a few minutes about the trust that is given to all those who handle animals, and then he went on to lead the prayers. Among these was one for horses and ponies which Angela thought was beautiful, and determined to learn by heart from the service sheet which she and Ian were sharing. Then everyone joined together to say The Lord's Prayer, the words sounding firm but thin in the open air, and the service ended with a blessing.

During the service the circle of horses remained almost still, as though they sensed the solemnity of the occasion. A few ears and tails twitched, and one or two impatient forefeet pawed the ground, but Magic and Moonshine stood like statues, their ears pricked, and the breeze stirring the braid in their manes. Once a donkey brayed, and an aircraft droned overhead, but the quiet spell remained until after the blessing, when the mounted stewards moved forward to take up their positions to lead the procession over the downs.

The procession was led by the horse-drawn vehicles, behind a steward, a girl riding a lovely grey horse. Magic and Moonshine were fourth in line, behind the coster pony. The Shires with their dray came after them, rumbling round the road until everyone reached the place where all the vehicles turned to commence the real procession. This would take them back past the place from which there would be a commentary given over more loud-speakers, then round the inside of the famous Derby turn at Tattenham Corner.

Coming down towards the commentator and the stewards who were handing out the rosettes, Ian and Angela could see the spectators packed solid in two deep rows on either side of the road. Magic and Moonshine pricked their ears and arched their necks, lifting their knees high like hackney ponies, and showing off as hard as they could. Uncle Arthur had a job to hold them in as the coster pony ahead pulled up for his driver to receive his rosette.

'And now we have Magic and Moonshine,' said the lady commentator. 'They are with us every year, and I always look forward to seeing them. Mr Perry has them in harness for the first time this year, and what a delightful turn-out it is; two cream Shetland ponies to a half-sized landau. I think I've only once seen a carriage like this before. Aren't they going well, and aren't they proud of themselves?'

Magic and Moonshine certainly were. They

paused impatiently while Uncle Arthur received his blue rosette from a smiling steward, and then they were off at a brisk, gay trot, down the gently sloping road between the lines of people and past the clicking cameras and gasping children. Angela felt herself go scarlet under all the attention, but Ian was staring straight ahead, and it struck Angela that he seemed almost bored by it all.

At the end of the racecourse road, when Uncle Arthur slowed up the ponies and took them on to the grass, he and the ponies and carriage were immediately surrounded by people. They all wanted to pat Magic and Moonshine, and ask questions about them, and the ponies 'asked' for sugar, and did some of their 'yes' and 'no' tricks as Uncle Arthur gave them the signals. The big Shires came crashing past a few paces away with their empty dray, and Uncle Arthur waved to his friend on the driving seat. Behind the last vehicle a seemingly endless stream of ridden horses began to come down the road, and after watching for a few minutes Uncle Arthur said that it was time they took the ponies back to the van and fed them.

They were unharnessing the ponies when the

dray driver came over to speak to them. His four great horses were already loaded into the brewery horse box, and the dray had been run-up on to its trailer behind.

'About what you were saying, over losing your stabling,' he said, as Uncle Arthur looked up from unfastening Magic's traces. 'I might be able to help you. We're a team short in our stables at the moment, and we will be for another month or so at least. I reckon I might get you in there for a time. I'll have a word with the stable foreman if you like. We're not so far from your place.'

'Would you really? That's awfully good of you.' Uncle Arthur's face went even redder. 'It really would be a load off my mind. It'd give me more time to find something permanent.'

'I'll do that, then,' promised the driver. 'Be a shame if you had to part with these two. Quite an eyeful, they are.'

He rubbed Moonshine and Magic behind the ears, his hand big and firm and used to the great mass of the Shires, but both ponies pricked their ears and breathed at him in a friendly way. When he had gone Uncle Arthur turned to Grace and the children in great excitement.

'Well,' he said. 'Fancy that. I do hope he can get us in. Be a real relief, that, wouldn't it?'

'Won't they feel awfully small among all those huge horses?' asked Angela. Uncle Arthur laughed.

'Soon get used to it,' he said. 'It won't bother them, they're cheeky enough for anything. But my word, won't it be nice to get them fixed up, even if it is only temporary.'

And as they collected their lunches and the ponies' feeds from the van, and led them away to find a quiet spot in the warm, pale golden September sunlight, they all, including Ian, hoped very hard that the driver of the dray really could provide Magic and Moonshine with a temporary home.

3 · Among the giants

For the three days following Horseman's Sunday everyone at Uncle Arthur's lived in a state of great anxiety, waiting to hear some news from the brewery stable. School had started again, and each day Angela and Ian hurried home to see if there had been a message or a letter. Although Ian could not manage to feel quite so concerned about the ponies as Angela, he knew how much it would upset everyone else if they had to go. And really, when he honestly thought about it, he did not want them to go for good himself.

On Wednesday afternoon the shop was closed, and so Angela and Ian went in the back way, through the yard and past the stable. Magic whinnied to them as he heard their steps, but today they were in too much hurry to find out if there was any news, and they did not stop as they usually did. Uncle Arthur and Grace were both in the living-room, and with them was Uncle Arthur's friend from the brewery stables. All three of them looked round and smiled at the children as they hurried in. Angela looked anxiously from face to face and knew at once it was all right. Uncle Arthur's face was red and beaming, and Grace looked happy.

'Hello kids,' said Uncle Arthur, rubbing his hands together. 'Good news. There's room for us at the brewery stables; the lads can move in on Saturday.'

'Oh good.' Angela dropped her school satchel on the settee and went to hug her Uncle. 'Oh, I am glad. So they won't have to go, not now, will they?'

'Well, not for two months, anyway,' Uncle Arthur sounded a little less light-hearted. 'But a lot can happen in two months.'

'And it might be a bit more,' put in his friend, who had in front of him a cup of tea and a plate with a slice of Grace's home-made fruit cake on it.

'Jolly good. I'm glad it's all right,' said Ian, rather less whole-heartedly. Angela was standing close to Grace, and Grace had put an arm casually round her as she talked. Again vaguely, Ian felt the odd one out. Of course, he was too old to want Grace to put her arm round him, that was for girls, anyway, but Angela seemed so very much at home with Grace and Uncle Arthur. She seemed so much more able really to take part in their lives, with her complete enthusiasm for the ponies, and her interest in the domestic things that Grace did, like cooking, and the knitting that Grace had recently started to teach her. And she liked playing the piano. Grace had started to give them both lessons, but Ian had not been very keen, and he had given it up very quickly. And in spite of all these things that he did not really feel keen about he had nothing special of his own to take their place. Standing there, he felt distinctly left out.

Then Grace looked round and noticed him, and asked him if he would like some tea and cake. The way that she said it made it obvious that she considered him almost one of the adults, and as he went to fetch himself a cup Ian did feel slightly better.

Uncle Arthur's friend, whose name was Bill,

went out to the yard with them before he left, and had a look at the ponies. He grinned at the sight of the stable and its miniature occupants, and said that it would certainly be a change for them at the brewery. Then he drove off in his clean and shiny Austin van and Uncle Arthur turned to the children.

'Well, we'll have to get started,' he said. 'Must have all their stuff spotless by Saturday. They go in for a bit of spit and polish in those stables, you know. We don't want them thinking we can't do as well.'

Uncle Arthur meant what he said. By Saturday he and the children had cleaned and polished every bit of leather, brass, and steel that the ponies possessed. The harness shone, the head collars and the little bridles were supple and gleaming, the lead reins that were used to take the ponies for walks in hand, and the long lunge reins on the end of which they were exercised were scrubbed and whitened. The carriage was washed and polished, and the feed and water buckets were scrubbed out. Grace made a few mild objections to the amount of time her sink spent filled with hot, soapy water while webbing reins and grooming brushes soaked, but she did not really mind. In fact, she did quite a bit of scrubbing and polishing herself.

Uncle Arthur did not forget the van in all these preparations. He brought it up to the gate at the back of the yard, swept all the straw out of it, and hosed it down both inside and out, before leaving it with the ramp down to dry. Curious neighbours paused to comment, and nearly all of them were horrified to learn that the ponies had got to move.

'Why, they're no trouble, never have been,' said one lady, who lived across the cinder path from Uncle Arthur's gate. 'We hardly ever hear them, and we don't even smell them unless the weather's really hot and you've been clearing out that muck heap.'

'Young fellow wants his head examined,' remarked another neighbour. 'Lowering the tone indeed. What about old Charlie Rogers and his rag-and-bone barrow? Leaves it parked right out in the path he does, too, smelly old thing that it is. What does that young chap think he's got to sell, Buckingham Palace?'

'Oh, he's out to get the best price he can, you can't blame him for that,' said Uncle Arthur forgivingly. 'It won't be so bad if I can get them fixed up somewhere near.'

All the neighbouring children, too, were sorry to see Magic and Moonshine moving out. Many of them had always come to visit the ponies frequently, bringing them gifts of titbits saved by their mothers for the purpose, and they would miss them very much.

'Perhaps they won't be far away for long,' Uncle Arthur told them encouragingly, and Angela hoped that it was true, and he was not just saying it to cheer everyone up, including himself. But it was not a cheerful moment when the ponies were loaded, and Uncle Arthur raised the ramp behind them to drive them down the cinder path for the last time.

Angela and Ian went with Uncle Arthur and the ponies to their new stables, but Grace had to stay behind to look after the shop. It was about five kilometres from Uncle Arthur's shop to the brewery, and some of the roads were very busy. But the brewery itself was at the end of a quiet side street. From the front, as they drove towards it, it seemed to be enormous and rather forbidding, a high, blank looking, red brick building with the name of the brewers,

'Champney's', in tall gold letters above a pair of high, wrought-iron gates. These stood open this morning, and as Uncle Arthur slowed the van ready to turn in they all saw one of the delivery wagons coming out. It was different from the one they had seen at Horseman's Sunday, just a flat platform without sides, piled high with crates; the driver sat high above the horses on a small, fragile-looking seat with a tall handbrake sticking up at his side. The horses were a pair of the magnificent black Shires, and they were moving at a slow jog trot, their great necks arched and the long white feathers on their legs flashing in the autumn sunlight.

At the sound of their hooves Magic whinnied, and peeping through the little window behind the driver's cab Angela could see him standing there in the dim interior. His tiny ears were very pricked, and his eyes shone. Angela knew that he was excited, and eager to know where they were going.

Through the gates the van was immediately stopped by the gatekeeper, who came out of a low brick building marked 'Inquiries', and held up his hand like a policeman. Uncle Arthur explained who they were and where they were going, and the gatekeeper grinned.

'I thought you'd strayed from a circus,' he said. 'OK, carry straight on, and you'll find yourselves at the stables.'

The main way through the brewery led past a maze of side turnings and blank-fronted buildings with big double doors and raised brick-built loading bays. Through some of the doors they saw pipes and cooling equipment, large vats, and a place for washing bottles.

Little metal tracks like miniature train tracks came out of other buildings, and down narrow side turnings, and they saw a man pushing a string of small metal barrels down one of these. Crates and barrels were stacked everywhere, and motor lorries were parked here and there at loading bays, waiting for their loads. There was also another wagon being loaded, the two black horses standing like statues, except for their nodding heads and ears as they chewed at their bits. Cats lurked among the crates and peered from doorways, and Uncle Arthur said that he betted there were plenty of mice about for them to catch. Over the whole place hung the smell of brewing, rich and sweet and full, making the children feel hungry, and Uncle

Arthur remark that he could do with a pint. And then they crossed another main roadway, and found themselves at the stables.

The stable building was in the shape of an E without the middle arm, and the centre part was in two storeys. In the yard were parked the spare wagons, and two drays with sides like the ones they had seen at Horseman's Sunday. A man was sweeping water down the yard towards a central drain, but as the van stopped he propped his broom against the wall and came to meet them.

'We've been expecting you,' he said. 'I'm Pat Massey, the stable foreman.'

Mr Massey was big and rather fat, with grey-brown hair and a dusty-looking face, but his blue eyes were very bright. He was dressed in an ancient grey pullover on top of a faded blue shirt, and his old grey flannel trousers were held up by an enormous, shiny leather belt with big silver studs and a large gilt buckle.

'Bill's away at the show,' he explained. 'But you come with me and I'll show you where your two monsters are to go.'

Uncle Arthur, Angela, and Ian followed Mr Massey across the cobbled yard to where a flight of steep, twisting stone stairs led up-wards. Beside them was the entrance to a rather dark, cobbled ramp. They all clattered up the stairs, and at the top they found themselves at one end of the long upper stable. The top of the ramp came out close by.

'This is where we keep the show horses,' explained Mr Massey over his shoulder. 'The working horses are downstairs.'

'Don't they all work, then?' asked Ian, surprised.

'No. They do a few years of travelling the shows, and then move on to the round,' Mr Massey told him. 'From May to October it's often practically empty up here. We travel them all over the country, showing in trade and heavy-harness classes, and in Shire breed classes. Then they give displays at agricultural shows, and at the 'Horse of the Year Show' at Wembley. And they do their bit in processions, the Lord Mayor's Show is usually our last big engagement of the year.'

'It doesn't sound so very much different to our game,' said Uncle Arthur, and Mr Massey said that he didn't suppose it was, except for the matter of size.

A wide gangway ran the length of the stable, with big stalls along either side of it. Light came in through high, clean windows on both sides, and the cobbled gangway was swept very clean. The stalls were deeply bedded down with a mixture of peat and wood shavings, and the green and white paintwork gleamed. There were enough stalls for twelve horses, six down either side, but only four were actually occupied. The great, dark hindquarters and thick, glossy black tails of these made Angela feel very small. Big, kind heads turned to look at them, and two of the horses greeted Mr Massey with a soft whicker.

'Midnight and Bomber,' said Mr Massey. 'They'll be due to retire from showing this autumn, they've done their bit of trailing round the country. You might not believe it, but it's a lot harder on them showing than doing the steady work on the round.'

'Is it really?' asked Ian.

'Yes, too many changes, no regular routine,' explained Mr Massey. 'These other two down here are younger. Dandy's only a four year old, we're still breaking him in, and Clover's five. She's been with us a year now, haven't you, old girl?'

He went up to give the big horse a friendly slap on the neck, and Angela and Ian gazed almost in awe at the first Shire horse they had seen close to, from ground level.

'How big is she?' asked Ian.

'Just under eighteen hands,' replied Mr Massey. 'She's not our biggest, not by quite a way. The record here at present is just under nineteen hands, one hand bigger.'

Clover looked quite big enough to Angela. Mr Massey was beckoning them into the stall beside her, but Angela hung back, although Ian went in quickly enough.

'It's all right, she won't hurt you. She's as gentle as a kitten,' said Mr Massey, but Angela was not convinced. Ian, however, thought the big horse wonderful. This was a real horse, not a toy, like the ponies. Just standing there she radiated power, and when Ian put his hand on her shoulder, as high up as he could reach, he could feel the swell of huge muscles under the warm, silky hair. Clover turned her head to look at him, and Ian held his hand out to her. Big, warm lips gently explored his hand, and a very long tongue licked the salt taste off his palm. Her head seemed half as long as Ian was tall,

but her eyes were very kind, and he found that
he was not at all afraid of her.

'She's lovely,' he told Mr Massey. 'Has she
won many prizes?'

'Oh, she's been in a good many prize-
winning teams,' replied Mr Massey. He
gave Clover a pat. 'Well, we'd better get on.

This isn't getting your animals settled, is it?'

He led the way out of the stall, and Angela looked admiringly at Ian.

'Weren't you scared of her?' she asked him, as they followed the two men on down the stable. 'She's so big.'

'She's gentle, though,' said Ian. 'But she's terrific, Angie. She feels strong, just standing there. She really is a horse.'

Then they saw that Mr Massey had stopped at the two end stalls on the left. These had fresh but rather more shallow beds of peat and shavings down in them, and Mr Massey said, 'Here you are. Will these be large enough, do you think?'

Uncle Arthur laughed. 'One of them would almost do us,' he said. 'They'll think they've come to live in a palace.'

'How will you shut them in?' asked Angela. 'Or will they have to be tied up all the time, like the others?'

'Oh, they'll have to put up with being tied,' replied Uncle Arthur. 'They won't mind, they'll have long ropes and plenty of room. All right to bring them up now?' he asked Mr Massey.

'Yes, soon as you like,' agreed Mr Massey.

Magic and Moonshine were delighted to be out of the van, and they gazed around them with great interest. Mr Massey grinned at the sight of them.

'Little all right, aren't they?' he said. 'You'd better mind none of the big fellows eats them up for breakfast.'

'Old Magic would give them indigestion if they tried,' replied Uncle Arthur laughing.

Angela had wondered if Magic and Moonshine would mind the ramp, but they did not seem in the least worried by it. Uncle Arthur went up first with Magic and Ian followed with Moonshine. Angela came behind carrying two hay nets, one slung over each shoulder.

The four big horses in the upstairs stalls turned interested heads at the sound of Magic and Moonshine's little hooves clattering on the cobbles, and Clover whinnied. Magic whinnied back in his usual cheeky way, and Uncle Arthur said, 'Now, now. You'd better mind what you say, my boy, until you've been here for a bit.'

'Do you think they really say something, or are they just making a noise?' asked Angela, as they reached the ponies' stalls.

'Oh, they say something, I'm sure,' replied

Uncle Arthur. 'That was probably "Who on earth are you?" and I bet Magic answered "Mind your own business".'

The two little ponies did look rather dwarfed by the big stalls with their high, solid partitions. They could not look over, and they had to stand facing the mangers, tethered by their head collar ropes. These were threaded through brass rings on the mangers and then through small blocks of wood known as 'logs', which dangled on the rope, preventing it from being pulled through the ring, and also holding it straight, so that it could not tangle round the ponies' legs. All the Shires were tethered in this way, but it was not good enough for Magic. He objected strongly to not being able to see what was going on, and he began to paw the ground and jerk his head up and down, banging his log against the brass ring. Dandy began to move restlessly in sympathy, and the other three pricked their ears. Mr Massey appeared to ask what was going on.

'Cheeky little shrimp,' he exclaimed, when Uncle Arthur explained. 'So our stables don't suit him, eh?'

'He'll settle.' Uncle Arthur did not want

57

Magic to make a bad impression, but Mr Massey did not seem to be cross.

'Better let him have his way,' he said. 'There are some old bales out at the back. We'll sling a couple of those up for them, if you'll give me a hand.'

'Bales' turned out to be heavy old doors, slung on their sides from two chains which fitted over the tops of the stall partition poles. Chains at the bottom also fitted to hooks in the floor, and Mr Massey and Uncle Arthur hung the bales low enough to prevent either pony trying to crawl under. With these in position across the open end of the stalls the ponies could be left loose, and Magic immediately hung out over his, eagerly gazing round his new home.

'We used to use those when we had a few lighter horses up here, vanners,' explained Mr Massey. 'The Shires are too big to leave loose in an ordinary single stall. They wouldn't be able to turn round safely, and they might get themselves cast.'

'What's that?' asked Angela, forgetting to be shy in her interest.

'Cast? That's what it's called when a horse lies down or falls, and gets itself stuck, unable to get up again,' explained Mr Massey. 'A horse can't get up unless it's got room to get its legs in the right position. If it's too close to a wall or on a slope it may get "cast".'

'Oh, I see.' Angela imagined one of the big Shires unable to get up, and struggling. It was rather a frightening thought. Handling a frightened Shire horse would be a very different thing from dealing with Magic or Moonshine.

4 · Settling in

By now it was almost half past twelve. Down in
the mews they could hear the clatter and rum-
ble of the drays beginning to come in, for Saturday was a short day, and work stopped for the
horses at one o'clock. None of the work horses
came upstairs, but Ian and Angela went down
with Uncle Arthur and Mr Massey to be shown
the feed room, and to collect Magic and Moonshine's dinners, and found the yard full of
them.

One pair was just being led into the stable by
one of the stablemen and their driver, their harness still on them with the long traces neatly
looped up. A second pair stood in the centre of
the yard, still hitched to their empty dray.
There was a light sheen of sweat on their necks
and flanks, and one of them lowered his head to

rub his big nose on his knee. Ian paused to watch the men unharness them, but Angela stayed beside Uncle Arthur, feeling safer well away from the big feet and great silken-haired legs.

'Bit big for you, aren't they?' said Uncle Arthur, and Angela admitted that they were.

The way to the feed room led through the central stable, past a large double stall in which stood the biggest horse that Angela and Ian had ever seen. He was kept in just by a rope slung between him and the gangway.

'My goodness,' exclaimed Uncle Arthur, stopping to marvel. 'That arrangement wouldn't keep either of mine in for a moment.'

'Do you think he bites?' asked Angela nervously, for the horse was leaning over his rope, and his huge head and neck extended the whole way across the gangway.

'Admiring Big Ben?' asked Mr Massey, catching up with them after pausing to speak to one of the men. 'One of the biggest horses in England he is, nearly nineteen hands tall.'

'So he's . . .' Ian did some rapid mental arithmetic. 'He's one hundred and ninety centimetres tall.'

'That's right,' agreed Mr Massey. 'At the point of his withers, that is. His neck's a lot higher, of course.'

'And Magic's only ninety-six centimetres tall,' said Uncle Arthur. 'That's quite a difference.'

Mr Massey laughed, and agreed that it was.

'And does that bit of string really keep him in?' asked Uncle Arthur, looking back at Big Ben's stall.

'His rope, you mean?' Mr Massey came past them and gave Ben a ringing, friendly slap on his enormous neck. 'Oh yes, old Ben won't come out. He's quite happy in there, cadging tit-bits from everyone who goes past. He knows he'd lose his privileges if he started getting out.'

'Does he bite?' asked Angela.

'Bite? Not Ben.' Mr Massey let the horse lip his hand, and Ben's lips moved over his outstretched palm as gently as Magic's did. Angela, though, was not convinced. She felt as though the horse would only have to open his mouth to bite her head right off, but she followed Mr Massey and Uncle Arthur timidly past him, and through the door into the harness room beyond. Ian paused to pat Ben, thrilled by the immense size and power of the magnificent animal, and Ben lipped his hands just as gently as he had Mr Massey's.

'This is the show horses' harness,' Mr Massey was explaining, when Ian joined them. They were in a big room with a large stove against one wall, and pegs and racks holding harness all around them. Everything was polished to a brilliant shine, leather and brass glowed in the shadows, against the white-washed walls, and a glass case across the centre of the room protected several sets of especially beautiful harness. There were two big photographs on the walls, one of a team of six Shires in the show ring, pulling a dray, and one of a team pulling a coach in the Lord Mayor's Show. Several pegs were empty, and Mr Massey explained that they belonged to those horses who were away at the shows.

'We keep the working harness at the other end,' he added. 'There wouldn't be room for it all in here.'

'There must be some work in keeping this lot clean!' exclaimed Uncle Arthur, and Mr Massey agreed that there was.

'Never finished here, that's us,' he said. 'Start at six, finish at six, twelve hour day, and we still don't always get through without extra time.'

But he sounded quite happy about it, and it was obvious that Mr Massey was content with his job.

The feed room was beyond the harness room, through another door, and was lined with big, galvanized bins. There were several sacks of carrots in one corner, and a pile of bundles of rich looking green-stuff, obviously freshly delivered. Uncle Arthur emptied the two sacks of fodder that he had brought into an empty bin, and then started to measure out Magic and Moonshine's midday feeds. Mr Massey grinned as he watched.

'That wouldn't go far with ours,' he said. One bite, that's about all.'

'How much do they eat a day?' asked Ian.

'Oh, about ten bucketsful each,' replied Mr Massey, and Ian thought for a moment that he was joking. Then he realized that the stable foreman was quite serious.

'Ten buckets?' exclaimed Uncle Arthur. 'And how much hay?'

'We don't feed hay,' explained Mr Massey. 'It makes a lot of extra work and litter, and doesn't give much return in nourishment that can't be given in short feed.'

'But don't they get bored with no hay to chew at?' asked Ian, remembering the hours that Magic and Moonshine spent in contented munching.

'They get green meat at night,' replied Mr Massey. 'In season, that is. In winter they have mangels to chew. And we feed them as many carrots as they'll eat before they go out in the morning. Then it takes them quite a while to work through their four or five buckets of short feed each evening.'

'I'll bet it does,' exclaimed Uncle Arthur, while Angela tried to imagine Magic faced with five buckets of food.

'When do they have the rest?' asked Ian

'They have two in the morning, before work,' replied Mr Massey. 'A nosebag while they're out, then about three buckets when they come in and the rest in the evening. We feed a mixture of maize, bran, chaff, and oats. They don't go hungry, I can tell you.'

Back upstairs with feeds for Magic and Moonshine they found that several of the drivers had gone up to look at the new arrivals.

Magic and Moonshine were leaning over their bales, and Magic was showing off some of his tricks, asking with one front foot, offering to shake hands, and doing part of one of his dances. This was a sort of rumba, in which Magic swung his hindquarters from side to side and jiggled his hind legs, and it was raising quite a laugh from his audience.

'Quite a clown, isn't he?' said one of the men, as Magic stopped dancing to whinny to Uncle Arthur. 'Can he do anything else?'

'Plenty.' Uncle Arthur put down the buckets, and proceeded to put both ponies through more of their tricks. He made them both bow, and he talked to Moonshine until Magic pretended to be jealous, and leaned out to nudge him. Then he turned his back on Magic and the pony quietly took a handkerchief from his back pocket while Uncle Arthur pretended not to know what was going on. The men laughed, and patted the ponies, but it was clear that they did not take them seriously. They thought that Magic and Moonshine were just pets, like tiny dogs, and not capable of doing any real work. In fact, one of the drivers did say laughingly that Champney's was turning into a circus, with Magic and Moonshine in the stables. When they had gone, and the ponies were eating, Angela said, 'They didn't think much of Magic and Moonshine, did they?' She was rather hurt. She was used to people admiring the ponies, not thinking them useless and rather funny, for she did not think that they were useless at all.

'Well, they are a bit small, aren't they?' said Ian, who rather shared the men's point of view. 'After all, they aren't really working animals.'

'They work jolly hard,' exclaimed Angela, stung. 'Look how much time they have to spend standing about in uncomfortable corners in theatres when the pantomimes are on, and look how they get driven about the country to appear at fêtes and shows in the summer. Even Mr Massey said shows were hard work. And they go beautifully in harness, they never try to be lazy.'

'But it still isn't real work, not like pulling those drays, or ploughing a field,' Ian pointed out. 'What they do isn't really a job, it's not important.'

'Of course it is. Look how many people have

said how much they enjoy watching them,' retorted Angela. 'And Uncle Arthur's told us that Shetland ponies are very strong for their size, and up to a terrific lot of work. They pull all of us in the carriage, don't they?'

But Ian still thought that, compared to the Shires, Magic and Moonshine were like toys, and not really very much more use.

When they got home, rather late for lunch, Grace was very eager to hear how Magic and Moonshine liked their new home, and she was glad to be told that they seemed quite contented. Ian told her about the Shires, and all that Mr Massey had said about the way they were looked after, and he was surprised to find afterwards that he had talked almost all through the meal. But Grace did not seem to have been bored, she asked questions, and really listened to what he said, and she seemed to have enjoyed listening as much as he had enjoyed telling.

Of course, having the ponies three miles away instead of in the backyard would mean a lot of extra work. Uncle Arthur would have to go over to the brewery stables early every morning to muck out and feed the ponies, and if he came home later in the morning he would have to return at lunch time to feed them, for he did not want to ask for any help from Mr Massey and his busy staff. Then he would have to go over again in the evening to feed them and settle them for the night. And there was still their exercising to be fitted in, either by driving them in the carriage, or lunging them somewhere as he often did on the recreation ground near the shop. It would mean that Grace must spend more time in the shop, and try to fit in the piano lessons she gave at times when she knew Uncle Arthur would be at home. In fact, it was not an ideal way to keep them, but for the time being they all knew that they would manage somehow.

The first complete day that the ponies spent at the brewery was a Sunday, a very quiet day for the Shires. They did not go out at all, and only Mr Massey and a few of the stablemen came in to do the essential feeding and mucking out. After seeing to the ponies in the morning Uncle Arthur, Ian, and Angela got home in time to go to church with Grace as they usually did. Then, while she finished cooking the dinner, they dashed over to give the ponies their feeds, and after they had been home for their own dinners Uncle Arthur, Grace, and Angela went back to take the ponies for a drive. Ian, however, did not go. He had arranged to play football with some school friends on the recreation ground, and although Angela missed him it was better than knowing that he was with them and feeling bored. Although why he should be bored with the ponies she did not know.

It was rather a grey sort of afternoon, with a slight mist about, and the streets were very quiet. Both Grace and Angela drove the ponies for a bit, and the eight little hooves tapped briskly along the empty Sunday streets and echoed sharply back from the tall, grey houses and the long, sooty terraces. In one overgrown square garden someone was burning leaves, and the sharp, tangy smell of the smoke drifted across their faces as the ponies trotted past. They all arrived back at the stables with glowing faces and tangled hair, and the sound of the ponies' hooves on the cobbles was greeted by a whinny from one of the resting Shires inside the stable.

As she helped Grace and her uncle to put the warm, prick-eared ponies away in their box-stalls and feed them Angela wondered how Ian could bear to miss such an afternoon. But when they got home Ian was just coming down the street, his football boots slung round his neck, and mud on his legs, shorts, and face, and he insisted that his afternoon had been just as good as theirs.

'Don't you like the ponies any more?' Angela asked him later, when they were alone in the sitting room for a few minutes.

'Oh, I like them,' said Ian. 'But I don't need to spend all my time with them, do I? The rest of you do that anyway.'

'Well, why not? They're fun, and I like helping with them,' Angela told him.

'So do I, in reason.' Ian felt cross. He had enjoyed his game of football in a way, but he could not help feeling that once again he had been left out of the family. The fact that it had been his own choice did not help. 'But they're only like toys really, aren't they? It's all right for you, you're younger, and anyway, you're a girl.'

'I don't . . .' began Angela, but then Grace came back into the room, and she stopped. Ian would only be cross if she let Grace hear them arguing about it, but she wished that she could understand why Ian seemed so touchy these days, and why he was no longer so keen on Magic and Moonshine.

On Monday morning the atmosphere at Champney's was very different. When Angela and Ian got there with Uncle Arthur, just before eight o'clock, after a very early breakfast, work was in full swing. Grace had not been very happy about them going to the stables before school, but they had both pleaded to go, and Uncle Arthur had promised to see that they had a good wash and got off to school in good time, and so she had given in.

Downstairs in the working horse section of the stables men were bustling in all directions, mucking out, carrying bags of shavings, or buckets of water, and starting to groom the big horses. Upstairs it was a little quieter, but the six horses who had been away showing had returned the previous evening, and all the stalls were full. Magic was leaning out over his bale, watching the coming and going of the two men who were mucking out up there, and he greeted Uncle Arthur and the children with a shrill, greedy whinny.

'Yes, I know it's breakfast time,' Uncle Arthur told him. 'But mucking out first.'

Ian helped him with this job while Angela began to brush Moonshine. Then, when the ponies had been fed and Uncle Arthur had started to groom Magic, he wandered away to

watch the men working on the Shires. Now that really was grooming, he thought, watching one of the men at work on Bomber, a massive black horse with long white stockings on all four legs. The soft body brush skimmed across the shining black coat with a rhythmic, circular movement, the evenness of each stroke almost hiding the amount of weight that the man was putting into the job. At the end of each sweep of the brush the man scraped it across the metal teeth of the curry comb that he held in his other hand, and all the time he kept blowing a steady 'sss' sound between his teeth to keep the dust out of his mouth. Then he turned to tap the grease out of the curry comb on to the floor and saw Ian watching.

'Bit different to grooming your pets, isn't it?' he asked.

'He's bigger,' admitted Ian, who was not going to run Magic and Moonshine down to Champney's men whatever he might think himself. 'But we groom ours just the same way. How big is he?'

'Seventeen two, this one,' replied the man. 'Not one of the biggest, of course, but he's a fair size to work on.'

'I bet he's strong,' said Ian, gazing admiringly at the big, shining horse.

'He is that,' agreed the man. 'He'd bowl one of your little ones over and not know he'd done it.'

He turned back to his grooming, and Ian

went on watching. When the man turned again to tap out his curry comb Ian said, 'Could I have a go, do you think? At grooming him, I mean?'

'Not scared?' the man grinned at him. 'He's got big feet, you know. You'd feel it if this one trod on your toe. And you'd need to put some weight behind the brush, no use tickling him.'

'I'm not scared,' Ian assured him. 'I'd love to try.'

'OK then.' The man handed the brush and curry comb to Ian and leaned back against the partition by the horse's head to watch. Ian stepped in beside the big horse, very conscious suddenly of the great height and mass towering above him. Bomber turned his great, gentle head and Ian stroked his nose. Then he slipped his hand through the canvas loop on the back of the brush, flattening his palm against the wooden back, and began to groom. Bomber stood quite still, and Ian concentrated on putting all his strength into each stroke of the brush. He was so occupied that he did not hear Uncle Arthur calling until the man said, 'They're wanting you. Time for school, I should think.'

'Are they?' Ian looked round, his face hot and crimson from the work. He tapped out the comb, finding quite a reasonable amount of grease in it, and the man looked quite impressed.

'Not bad,' he said. 'I didn't think you'd have an idea, but that wasn't bad at all. I can start the other side now.'

He gave Ian a friendly smile, and Ian felt quite proud of himself as he went to join Uncle Arthur and Angela. He might have made mistakes sometimes with the ponies, but he couldn't be so hopeless after all.

Angela and Ian washed in the small wash room downstairs, and brushed the hay and shavings off each other as best they could. Uncle Arthur said when they rejoined him that they had better wear something old next time, and change when the ponies were done.

'Otherwise the whole of your school will smell of horses, and then I'll have your teacher after me,' he said.

Most of the drays had gone out by the time Ian and Angela hurried out to catch the bus for school. Mr Massey had told them that the horses worked from eight thirty until three o'clock.

In that time each dray did about three deliveries of beer to local public houses owned by Champney's.

'They'll be back before we get here after school,' remarked Ian, as they dashed out of the gate.

5 · More like man's work

Angela and Ian went straight back to the stables after school. Angela was glad to find that Ian was as keen as she was to get back there. She had been afraid that he would want to do something else, and Uncle Arthur had said that she must not go alone, as she was not used to either the journey there or the big horses.

The drays were in now, as Ian had said they would be, standing idle in the yard, and the blacksmith was at work in the forge at the end of the left hand stable block. Uncle Arthur's blacksmith came round by van, and nailed 'cold' factory made shoes on to the ponies' hooves in the more usual modern way. Uncle Arthur sometimes shook his head over their feet, and said that shoeing wasn't what it used to be when every blacksmith had made his shoes

himself, but Angela and Ian had never seen this
done. Now they paused, fascinated, to watch,
for the brewery smith worked in this traditional
way, heating the metal in his coke fire and
hammering it into shape on the anvil. In the
shadows of the forge the fire glowed intensely
red, and when the smith placed the half-made
shoe against the hoof of one of the Shires to

check the fit, clouds of blue, acrid smoke blew out into the yard from the singeing horn.

'Doesn't it hurt him?' wondered Angela, gazing at the calm horse.

'No. You know Uncle Arthur said that there's no feeling in the horny part of their feet,' Ian reminded her.

When the shoe was shaped and fitted the smith plunged it into an iron tank of cold water with a tremendous sizzling noise, and then hung it with two others on the edge to cool while he started work on the fourth. He winked at the children over the fire as he pulled the handle to work the bellows, and they grinned back. Ian would have stayed to watch the shoes nailed on, but Angela pulled at his arm.

'Come on,' she said. 'We'd better find Uncle Arthur, and tell him we're here. He might want us for something.'

Rather unwillingly, Ian let himself be led away, but when they got upstairs they found Magic bridled ready for exercise and Uncle Arthur bending over one of Moonshine's front feet.

'Only shod two weeks ago, and this shoe's

loose already,' he told the children. 'That's cold shoeing for you.'

'The blacksmith's down in the forge now,' Ian told him. 'He's making the shoes himself, like you told us some smiths did. Couldn't he do something about it?'

'Is he?' Uncle Arthur brightened up. 'I'll go and have a word with him.'

The blacksmith agreed quite readily to fix Moonshine's shoe, and Uncle Arthur told the children to take the pony to him while he gave Magic his run on the exercise ground behind the stables.

The big Shire was just coming out of the forge when the children and Moonshine got there, stamping out behind one of the stablemen on his ringing new shoes. The smith was sweeping up, and he grinned when he saw Moonshine.

'Cor, what a little 'un,' he exclaimed. 'He wants to be stood up on stilts for this job. Still, let's have a look at him.'

Moonshine's hoof looked tiny in the smith's hard, smoke-stained hand, but he stood quite quietly while his shoe was nailed back on again.

'Rough old shoes, all the same, these factory

ones,' remarked the smith. 'You tell your uncle I'll make a decent set each for this fellow and his mate before they go.'

When Moonshine was finished the blacksmith showed them some of the shoes he had made ready for the big horses. There were hooks on the walls, with the names of the different Shires above them, and on some of these sets or odd new shoes hung ready. The smith took down one enormous shoe from Big Ben's peg, and handed it to Ian.

'Three kilograms, that weighs,' he said, smiling at Ian's startled face. 'Old Ben's a bit clumsy with his feet, and I shoe him extra thick. These'll last him seven or eight weeks.'

'It's huge,' exclaimed Angela. 'Moonshine's foot would go right through the middle of it.'

'Yes, there's quite a bit of iron in that shoe,' agreed the smith, hanging it back on its hook. 'Now, don't forget to tell your Uncle what I said about these little 'uns' next lot of shoes.'

Uncle Arthur was out at the back with Magic, lungeing him in circles at the end of a long white webbing lunge rein. There was also a big Shire out there, Dandy, the youngest of the show horses, being taught to walk quietly on a leading rein. It was Bill who was leading him, as he was not one of the delivery drivers, but worked mostly with the show horses. The children stopped with Moonshine on the edge of the big cinder-covered area to watch.

Out here, behind the stables, and cut off from the outside by a high brick wall, they might have been a hundred miles from London. Two tall elm trees in a corner shed drifts of golden leaves over the cinders, and the sun was bright and the light crystal clear. The air smelt of autumn leaves and damp ground, with the background richness of brewing, and a tang of horses. An old heavy breaking cart for training the young horses stood in the centre of the cinder yard, its wood mellowed to a golden brown colour.

Magic circled Uncle Arthur at a brisk trot, his neck arched and his ears pricked, his coat a warm cream colour against the dark cinders. Beyond him the big Shire moved ponderously, but playfully, tossing his head, and every now and then waltzing heavily sideways until Bill steadied him with a quiet word and a touch on the rein. Then Uncle Arthur called Magic in and patted him, and came to take Moonshine.

'Can I put Magic away?' asked Angela, and Uncle Arthur agreed that she could. Bill was coming in as well now, with Dandy, and Ian said, 'Could I help you with him, do you think?'

'Well, I don't know.' Bill looked slightly doubtful. 'He's a bit touchy, and you're a bit small to be around these big fellows, aren't you?'

'I helped groom Bomber this morning,' Ian told him.

'Did you now?' Bill smiled at him. 'OK, you come along with me. I daresay I can find you a job.'

In the end Ian spent the rest of the afternoon helping with the Shires. When Dandy had been brushed over and settled Bill took him down to the harness room, where two of the stablemen were at work on the show harness.

'Brought you a helper,' Bill told them. 'He'd like to have a go at some full sized harness for a change.'

Ian felt a bit shy, but he did want to help. At first the men teased him about the difference between Magic and Moonshine's 'fairy' harness, and their size, but soon they realized that he really did know something about cleaning harness, and did it quite well. Instead of teasing they began to offer advice, and to give him bits of their own sets of harness to clean, and Ian found that he had been accepted.

When the harness was done there were the late afternoon jobs around the stable to be attended to, and Ian helped to tidy up the stalls and check that all the automatic water bowls were filling properly. To start with the men kept an eye on him, not sure that he could move safely around the big horses, but Ian knew how to approach a horse. He knew that he must always speak to the horse before entering its stall, so that he did not startle it into kicking or shying, and that it was always safest to go round a horse under its head rather than round the tail. If he did have to go round behind a horse he remembered to keep close up to its back legs, with a hand on its tail, for a very close range kick was not dangerous, as there was no force in it. Also, keeping a hand on the horse told it where he was, and made it less inclined to move suddenly backwards. He and Angela had both learned these things from being around Magic and Moonshine, and watching the way that

Uncle Arthur handled them, and size made little difference when it came to things like that.

Angela and Uncle Arthur were ready to go before Ian had finished helping, and they had to go and find him.

'Hey, you're not taking our new stable boy away, are you?' asked Mr Massey, and Ian knew that he really had proved himself capable of being a help. As they drove home in the van he was feeling happier than he had for some time.

By the end of the first week it seemed to the children that the ponies had been at Champney's for ages. The journeys to the brewery from home and from school had already become familiar, and the routine of the big stable was becoming a part of their lives. Uncle Arthur still worried about finding new stabling for the ponies, but Ian, at least, was in no hurry for them to move. He found helping with the big horses the most absorbing, fascinating thing that he had ever done, and something that seemed to be entirely his own, for Angela was still very wary of them. Ian never grew tired of being close to their size and power, and he worked really hard to earn the approval of the men. For grooming, he often had to use the wooden steps which the men used for reaching the top of the biggest horses, like Big Ben, but he quickly became an expert at nipping on and off them, and none of the horses played up.

The only horse that Ian did not help with a lot was Dandy, but it was Dandy who seemed to have become Magic's special friend. The little pony always whinnied to the young Shire whenever Dandy went out or came in, and when Magic went out himself he would pause at Dandy's stall to whicker a greeting. Dandy always replied, turning his head as far as he could and pricking his ears at his small friend.

'Just so long as Dandy doesn't start trying Magic's tricks,' said Bill, watching the two whinny to each other one day. 'He's a bit big for shaking hands.'

'Trust Magic to find a friend,' said Uncle Arthur. 'At home he's got Partner, now he's picked Dandy. Moonshine never makes friends like that.'

At home, Partner was miserable without the ponies. He would wander into the empty shed, standing in the doorway and gazing round at the clean-swept boxes with a sorrowful expression on his face. Then he would turn away and go back into the house to curl up in a ball on a chair, or he would leap up on to the shed roof and sit there with his paws tucked under him, gazing out at the cinder path as though he was watching for Magic and Moonshine to come home.

Angela, too, hated seeing the empty shed, but to Ian life had become far more exciting and worthwhile now than it had been when Magic and Moonshine were in the yard.

'It must be jolly exciting, driving behind big horses,' he said one day to Bill. 'I always feel top heavy behind our two.'

'It's a good feeling,' agreed Bill. 'Although I wouldn't really have called it exciting. Our teams are pretty sedate, no rodeo stuff from any of them. Even young Dandy will calm down when he gets in the breaking cart beside something sensible like old Ben.'

'I'd love to go out on the round one day,' said Ian longingly.

'There's no reason why you shouldn't,' replied Bill. 'One of the men would take you along on a Saturday morning, I expect. Of course, you'd have to ask your Uncle first.'

Ian did ask, and Uncle Arthur agreed that he could go if one of the men would take him. Bill arranged for him to go with a driver called Frank, and Ian could hardly wait for next Saturday morning.

Angela was rather hurt by Ian's keenness on the big horses. Hurt on behalf of the ponies, that was. She felt that Ian was neglecting them, and when Ian had dashed off on Saturday morning to look for Frank she gave both ponies an apple to show that at least she had not abandoned them. Magic shook hands for his, and then kissed her for thank you, and Angela was quite unable to understand how Ian could prefer the big, clumsy black horses to the charming little ponies.

'Why doesn't Ian like Magic and Moonshine any more?' she asked Uncle Arthur rather miserably.

'Oh, he does, he does really,' Uncle Arthur assured her. 'He just wants to have a go at something that looks more like man's work than these two. Might have felt the same myself once, before I stopped worrying so much about what other people think. Though I do think Ian's really keen on those big horses, handsome fellows, you know, can't help admiring them myself.'

The Shires and their wagon were certainly a man's work. Just harnessing the two horses took all the height and strength of Frank and one of the stablemen, for one of the pair was Big Ben. His collar was an enormous thing, solidly-stuffed leather, with big brass guiding rings for the reins to run through, and big enough to slip over his big head and down his massive neck. His partner was Jasper, another big horse, although at eighteen hands he was eight centimetres shorter than Ben.

'Do the same pairs always go out together?' Ian asked Frank, as he walked out beside him and Big Ben.

'Mostly,' replied Frank. 'It takes a bit of time to match a good pair for height and pulling ability. It's no use putting a lazy one with a willing one, or the willing one does all the pulling while the other hangs back with slack traces and shirks. But if you put two lazy ones together someone's got to do the work, so most often they both will.'

'Are these two lazy?' Ian asked him.

'No, these are a good pair, good steady workers both of them,' replied Frank.

Outside Ian was thrilled at being allowed to hold Jasper while Big Ben was 'put too' or backed into his place on the right of the long wooden pole which divided the two horses. Frank linked up the traces to their rings and hooks, and then came back to take Jasper and back him into position on the other side of the pole. While Frank and the stableman worked Ian looked more closely at the wagon. It was very solidly built, a flat timber platform on a heavy timber frame, and the wheels had big rubber tyres on them. Ian had noticed that one of the other wagons in the yard was of a different type. Instead of having a solid platform it had bars with spaces between, and its wheels had iron rims instead of rubber tyres. The wheels, too, were set at an odd angle, leaning slightly outwards from where the rims touched the ground.

'That one?' said Frank, when Ian asked him why these wagons were different. 'That's one of the real old ones, one hundred and forty years old, that one is. We were using it up to this spring, but it finally had to be condemned. It's called a barrel dray, or an 'old roller', we used to call them, for the noise those iron wheels made.'

'Wasn't it much harder for the horses to pull, with iron tyres?' asked Ian.

'No, believe it or not those iron tyres ran easier, once they got it moving,' replied Frank. 'But rubber's better with a modern braking system.'

'How old is this wagon?' asked Ian, as Frank gave Jasper a pat before mounting the high seat.

'Oh, about forty years,' replied Frank. 'They're mostly about that. It's not easy to get a decent wagon built these days, there aren't the wheel-wrights about to do the job now that all the young chaps can have it easier in a factory. They don't care about being craftsmen these days, all they want is quick, easy money. Now, you jump up on the back with Dave, and we'll get loaded up.'

Dave was Frank's handler, who came along to help load and unload the crates, but who had nothing to do with the horses. He was a fair-haired, silent boy of about nineteen, dressed in jeans and a tough duffel jacket. He nodded at

Ian as he scrambled up, but did not speak. Frank climbed up on to the high, single driving seat, released the tall hand brake, and clucked to the two horses. The wagon began to move smoothly down the cobbled yard. Ian saw Angela and Uncle Arthur waving to him from the stairs, and waved back. His own private adventure had begun.

6 · Horse power

It took quite a long time to load the wagon up with crates of beer, but at last it was fully laden, and once again Ian climbed on to the back with Dave. A small space had been left for them between the crates, and under him Ian felt the wagon start to move again. They clattered down the wide, cobbled way between the brewery buildings towards the main gates, and Ian saw the tall buildings and the stacked crates slide slowly past. Then they were out into the quiet road, heading for the busy main street.

At the turning the horses came to a halt, but only for a moment. Then, at a word from Frank, they moved forward again, turning into the stream of traffic. Remembering how close to Magic and Moonshine cars sometimes came Ian felt rather nervous. This road was much busier than the ones that Uncle Arthur usually took them out on. Dave, however, seemed quite unconcerned; he was chewing a piece of gum, and staring out at the passing stream of cars, and soon Ian realized that there was no need to worry about the traffic. Cars and vans were eager to give them a wide berth, anxious not to risk their paint on any part of the heavy, slow-moving wagon, or to risk one of those huge hooves hitting any part of their vehicle.

Under Ian the wagon moved smoothly on its thick tyres, and in front, by peering round the crates, he could glimpse the big black hind-quarters and the high carried tails of the two horses. Hooves and jangling brasses made music in the midst of the noisy roar of traffic, and people on the pavements looked round and most of them looked pleased to see the living horses in the middle of all the metal and machinery. Jasper and Big Ben went at a slow jog, keeping a steady course, except for pulling out now and then to pass a parked car or van. Each change of direction was carefully signalled first by Frank's long whip.

Their load was for 'The King's Head', and almost before Ian had got properly used to the sensation of riding on the wagon Frank was bringing the horses to a halt outside. Dave stood up and hauled down the metal trolly that was

used to wheel in the crates, and Frank secured the horse's reins round the handbrake and dropped down to help.

'Shall I hold the horses?' asked Ian eagerly.

'Well, we usually have to trust them, but it would make us safer if you were to stand at their heads,' agreed Frank.

And so Ian went to stand by Jasper and Big Ben's heads while the wooden trap-door in the pavement was opened, and the two men began to wheel trolly loads of crates across to it. The two big horses lowered their heads to breathe at

Ian, and most of the passers-by paused to admire them. Ian felt very proud of them. He had helped to groom them and worked on their harness, he had driven behind them, and now he was at their heads. He had a share in them. It was a good feeling, and he stood very happily, stroking the big, soft noses until Frank and Dave had finished and once again the wagon was empty.

Going back was, if anything, more fun, because there was nothing in the way now to stop Ian from seeing the horses. Jasper and Big Ben knew that they were going home now, and perhaps even that it was Saturday, and a short working day. They went at an eager jog, the fastest that they were allowed to go on the hard roads in case of damaging their legs, their necks arched, and their ears pricked forward. In front of Ian the massive hindquarters rose and fell, and the traces lifted up and down above the horses' hocks to the rhythm of their jog. Above him Frank sat on the spidery driving seat as though it were a horse itself, his feet braced against the foot rest, and his shoulders squared as he held back his two tons of living engine power.

Watching him, Ian knew what he wanted to do himself when he grew up. It might be a queer thing to want to do in these days, to drive a team of heavy horses, but for the moment it was what Ian wanted. Of course, he knew that he might change his mind, as he had about driving a fire engine or being a professional footballer, but for the time being Ian could think of nothing finer than sitting up on that slender metal seat and driving the two immense horses home to lunch. And whether or not he did become a driver, Ian knew for certain that a strong love of the great horses was settled deep inside him, and that it, at least, would never change.

'Well?' inquired Uncle Arthur later, when Ian had finished helping Frank and the stableman to unharness and rub down Jasper and Big Ben. 'Did you enjoy yourself?'

'It was terrific,' replied Ian. 'And do you know, Frank says I can go out with them again next Saturday? Honestly Uncle, they're marvellous horses. They're such hard workers, and they're terrifically sensible. Do you know, the cars got out of our way this morning, instead of us having to get out of theirs? You can really respect horses like those.'

He continued to chatter eagerly about Jasper and Big Ben and his trip on the dray all the way home in the van, and all through lunch. Angela was inclined to be hurt because he so obviously thought them better than Magic and Moonshine, and even Uncle Arthur said half jokingly, 'Better keep quiet when you're with the lads, Ian, or they'll be jealous.'

'No they won't,' said Grace, as she got up to fetch the pudding. 'They know there's room for both the workers and the entertainers, and for the very big and the very small. They're much too sensible to be jealous.'

'Ian seems a lot happier these days,' she remarked to Uncle Arthur, that evening, after Ian and Angela were in bed.

'Yes, he does, I thought that,' agreed Uncle Arthur. 'It's those big horses, he's really keen on them. It's surprised me, the way he's taken to handling them. I wouldn't have thought he had it in him.'

'All Ian needed was a bit of confidence in himself as a person, apart from Angela and us,' replied Grace. 'Finding he can handle those horses, and getting interested in them, seems to have given it to him.'

Time passed very quickly for them all during the next few weeks. Ian and Angela's time was completely full, with school, the brewery stables, and homework, and Uncle Arthur seemed to be constantly dashing between the brewery and the shop in his gaily painted van. Grace did a bit of everything, the housework and the cooking, minding the shop, giving piano lessons, and going along when she could to join the rest of her family at the stables. Sometimes Ian and Angela did the shopping on their way from the bus stop to the brewery, but very often that had to be Grace's job too.

Although Ian was quite happy with things as they were even he had to admit that it made life rather hectic, and Angela knew that Uncle Arthur was growing more worried about the future. A lot of the time that the ponies were to stay at Champney's had passed now, and he was still no nearer to finding a stable for them. And it was clear that they could not go on rushing about as they were for too long. It had been simple enough to fit the ponies into the daily routine when they were in the back yard, but the distance to Champney's did make it much harder. Already Grace had lost one piano pupil because she had not had the time to give the child the extra lessons that she wanted. Also several times people had complained because they had been sent the wrong papers, after the rush in which Grace and Uncle Arthur had sorted them, and once or twice the shop had been closed when it should have been open. This meant that people coming to buy something found that they could not get it at Uncle Arthur's shop, and had to go somewhere else. All of this was very bad for business.

'We can't go on like this much longer,' said Uncle Arthur one evening, after an especially frantic day. 'I can't risk losing too many customers, and you don't want to lose any more pupils, Grace. We've got another three weeks or so at Champney's, this can't go on any longer than that, even if they offer to let us stay longer. We must find a handier solution somehow.'

'If there is one,' Grace pushed her long, slightly roughened fingers through her curly dark hair. 'I honestly think we've tried everything, Arthur.'

'The shop hasn't been sold yet, has it?' asked Ian. 'Mightn't the new landlord, when we get one, let Magic and Moonshine come back here?'

Uncle Arthur shook his head. 'Goodness knows,' he said. 'Can't rely on it, not by a long chalk. There must be something else, we've just got to keep looking.'

It was all rather depressing. Even Grace no longer seemed to be so optimistic.

'Surely Uncle Arthur will find somewhere, he couldn't ever sell them, could he?' Angela asked Ian, later that evening, when she and Ian were sitting on Ian's bed in the narrow room which was really half a room with a partition down the middle. On the other side of the partition Angela slept. They were both in their dressing-gowns, ready for bed, but Angela had felt too anxious to go straight to sleep.

'If he can't find anywhere, I don't see what else he can do,' replied Ian.

'Would you mind if they did go, really?' Angela asked him.

Ian looked down at the floor. Would he mind? A few weeks ago he would probably have said 'No', but now he was not so sure. After all, Magic and Moonshine were the same creatures as his beloved Shires, even if they were in miniature. And if it hadn't been for them he would not have had the knowledge to be accepted as a helper by the stablemen. He owed them that, and also, he realized, he was and underneath always had been fond of them for themselves. It was just that he had been feeling lost and left out, and had blamed the ponies for it, when it was not really their fault at all.

'Yes,' he said now. 'Of course I'd mind. And think how Uncle Arthur would feel. He just wouldn't know what to do without them.'

His answer made Angela feel quite a lot happier. At least Ian was on their side. She had hated it when she thought that he was not.

When Uncle Arthur and the children got home at tea time the next day Grace said that there was a message for Uncle Arthur from the theatrical agent who handled the bookings for the ponies. Uncle Arthur went to telephone him, and came back looking pleased.

'A job for the lads,' he told his family. 'Advertising a new film. We're to get ourselves up as a Victorian turn out, and plaster posters all over the carriage, then tour around hoping seeing us will make people want to see the film.'

'When?' asked Angela eagerly.

'Next Thursday and Friday afternoons,' replied Uncle Arthur. 'And then we're to be outside the cinema when the première begins on Saturday evening.'

'What, up in the West End?' exclaimed Grace.

'Yes, Leicester Square, no less,' Uncle Arthur told them. 'I'll take them up in the van, of course, too far to drive them at night anyway.'

'Can we come?' asked Angela.

'You can come along in the van,' replied Uncle Arthur. 'No costumes for you to wear in the carriage, though, and any case we're to give the actress who plays the star part a ride up to the cinema entrance. But you can certainly come in the van.'

'There was another thing, too,' Uncle Arthur said, a few minutes later, when the chatter about the première had died down. 'Quentin wanted to know about panto bookings. He said he'd had an inquiry about ponies for 'Cinderella on Ice' at the Empire Pool, Wembley, and he wondered if mine would be available. It'd be a good booking, have to have them specially shod, of course, but I said I'd let him know. No use accepting bookings for the new year before we've found a place to keep them.'

'But mightn't you lose it if you don't accept quickly?' asked Grace, who was handing round bread and butter. 'Wembley would be the biggest panto booking they've had, wouldn't it? I should accept it, I think, you'll manage somehow.'

'Maybe, maybe. I don't know. I'll give it until tomorrow, anyway,' said Uncle Arthur. 'Best not to rush into it at the moment.'

In the end, rather doubtfully, Uncle Arthur did take Grace's advice, and accepted the pantomime booking. Angela felt that it was a good omen. Surely now he would have to keep the ponies somehow, for she knew that Uncle Arthur would hate to break an agreement.

Preparing Magic and Moonshine and their carriage for the film advertisement created a lot of amusement among the men at Champney's. The advertising agency who had booked them provided Uncle Arthur with two big plywood frames bearing posters for the film, and a Victorian coachman's outfit for himself. On the first afternoon he would drive down to the embankment, and along the side of the river to the Battersea Festival Gardens. On the second he would drive the ponies in the van across the river, and drive them around Chelsea and Kensington.

The plywood frames fitted into the body of the carriage, so that the posters stood up clear of the low sides. Both Ian and Angela helped to harness Magic and Moonshine, as they had also helped to groom them. Even to Ian the little ponies were, for the moment, more interesting than the Shires. Uncle Arthur left the children holding the ponies while he went away to change into his costume. When he came back they could hardly recognize him. He wore tight scarlet knee breeches and white leggings with black buckle shoes. His coat was dark grey, with long tails. On his head was a tall black hat with a white band round it, and a white cockade sticking up at the side. He also wore a long, dark false moustache.

'You look lovely, Uncle Arthur,' Angela told him.

'Do I, do I?' Uncle Arthur looked pleased. 'Got to do the lads justice, you know.'

With Uncle Arthur in position on the driving seat the effect was both dramatic and eye-catching. Most of the stablemen gathered to see them off, and a pair of Shires coming in late pulled aside to make way for the little ponies. There was a ragged cheer from the men as the turn-out started off, and more men came to the doors of the store rooms and malt houses to watch as the ponies went by.

'Makes quite a show, does your Uncle,' said Mr Massey, as the little carriage went out of sight. 'Not found a new stable yet, has he?'

'No, not yet,' admitted Ian.

'Oh well, no hurry yet, so far as we're concerned,' said the stable foreman. 'We've had no news of the new pair coming, so he's got a while yet.'

Uncle Arthur's drive round London went very well, he told them when he got back. The ponies had behaved beautifully, and a lot of people had shown interest in them, as they could hardly help doing, thought Angela. Then, on Saturday evening, both ponies were loaded into the van, the carriage was run up on to the trailer, and they set out for the première in Leicester Square. Grace and the children went along as well, sitting up in the cab with Uncle Arthur as the van rumbled along the dark streets to the river, and drove on across the wide bridge, with the lights of London and the embankment coming up ahead of them, gleaming in the black water. Towards the West End the sky was a vivid pink as the clouds reflected the mass of lights, and they saw Big Ben's namesake lit up against the sky as Uncle Arthur drove along the embankment. Brightly lit trains crawled across Hungerford Bridge like yellow caterpillars, and as they turned away from the river towards the central theatre area of the West End the few people on the pavements became crowds.

Uncle Arthur parked the van in a quiet dark street on the edge of Covent Garden market. When they got down from the cab the children could smell oranges and cabbage, and the thousand other mingling smells of the big vegetable and fruit market, closed and silent now for the night.

'Better get them harnessed,' said Uncle Arthur. 'We haven't got too much time.'

Magic and Moonshine were excited by the strange place, and the nearby roar of traffic and the light at the end of the street. They snorted and tossed their heads, fidgeting so that Grace had to help hold them while Uncle Arthur and

Ian got them harnessed. When Uncle Arthur dressed in his coachman's outfit, stepped on to the seat they were immediately fretting to be off.

'All right?' asked Grace, still at their heads.

'Right,' agreed Uncle Arthur, and Grace let go and stepped back as the two little ponies jumped forward. The carriage lamps were lit, gleaming golden on either side, and shining on the creamy tails and hindquarters of the ponies as they came past Ian and Angela, breaking into a trot towards Charing Cross Road.

'Come on,' said Grace. 'We'll have to be quick if we want to be there before them. Arthur's only got to pick up Catherine Kerby, the actress, round the corner, and he'll be on his way to the cinema.'

She took Angela's hand, and with Ian hurrying alongside they set off in the wake of the ponies.

7 · Not a joke any more

There was a big crowd in front of the cinema in which the première was being held. A red carpet ran down the cinema steps and across the pavement to where the cars pulled up with the various stars and guests inside, and flood-lights shone out across the street towards the green gardens in the centre of the square. Grace and the children edged their way forward until they had a good view of the steps and the street. They were just in time.

Faintly, they heard the sound of trotting hooves through the roar of traffic and people began to stand on tip-toe and peer to see what was coming. Then Magic and Moonshine came into sight round the corner of the square, and a loud murmur went up from the crowd. Both ponies were trotting briskly, ears pricked, and necks arched, with Uncle Arthur above them on the driving seat, splendid in his grey and red costume. In the carriage itself sat Catherine Kerby, the star of the film, dressed in a gorgeous white dress under a peacock blue cloak trimmed with white fur. Her blonde hair was piled high on her head, and sparkled with shining jewels. Uncle Arthur brought the ponies round to the steps and they came to a flourishing halt right at the end of the red carpet.

'They look like fairy ponies,' whispered Angela, and certainly Magic and Moonshine hardly looked real. They were cream and silver under the big flood-lights, champing their bits and tossing their heads while the doorman helped their passenger to alight. There was a round of applause from the crowd as she started up the steps, and she turned for a moment to wave. Then she had vanished into the brilliantly lit foyer of the cinema, and Uncle Arthur was driving Magic and Moonshine on out of the square, away into the traffic and the hurrying crowds back to the quiet street and the waiting van. Grace and the children edged their way out of the crowd and began to hurry after them.

Back at the van Uncle Arthur already had the ponies unhitched, and he was starting to remove Magic's harness while Moonshine stood tethered to the van.

'Good, weren't they?' he said. 'Did they go down well, do you think?'

'They were wonderful,' Angela told him. 'They really looked lovely. Like fairy ponies.'

And she put her arms round Magic and kissed him on the nose.

Just how well the ponies' appearance had gone down was shown the next morning. Almost all the papers had a photograph of them outside the cinema, and one of their neighbours was round early to tell them that the ponies had been on television, in a late report of the première. Then, on Tuesday, Uncle Arthur received a letter. He read it, and then handed it to Grace.

'What do you think of that?' he asked her.

Angela and Ian watched, their eggs and bacon forgotten, while Grace read. They both knew from Uncle Arthur's voice that it was something serious. Then Grace looked up.

'It's a good offer,' she said. 'But you needn't accept it, surely? Not yet.'

'Well, not for a bit, perhaps,' Uncle Arthur had taken the letter back and was gazing down at it. 'But it'd be a good home for them. It's a big firm, they'd look after them well.'

'Uncle Arthur, what is it?' asked Angela urgently.

Uncle Arthur did not answer, but Grace said, 'It's from Swales and Lawrence, the department store people. They want a pair of ponies for advertising round London, like those grey horses that pull a carriage advertising Rothman's. They saw the reports about them at the première, and they think they sound just what they've been looking for.'

Angela and Ian did not know what to say. Suddenly, the ponies' going for good seemed terribly close. Angela looked down at her plate, and found that she did not want any more bacon and egg, and from the way that Uncle Arthur had begun to push his bacon about with a fork, neither did he. Grace looked round at them, and decided that things needed cheering up.

'It hasn't come to accepting anything yet,' she said briskly. 'There's still plenty of time.

Now, eat up your bacon, and does anyone want another cup of tea?'

But however much Grace might try to be cheerful Angela knew that she was not much more optimistic than the rest of them about Magic and Moonshine's future.

In the end Uncle Arthur wrote back to Swales and Lawrence thanking them for their offer and saying that he would like to think it over. But there was a shadow over everything that they did, and even to Ian the brewery stables seemed suddenly less fun.

The next Saturday Angela and Ian stayed on at the stables alone to finish grooming the ponies while Uncle Arthur hurried back to look after the shop while Grace gave a piano lesson. They were hard at work, Angela on Moonshine and Ian on Magic, when they heard Bill take one of the Shires out. Magic turned round in his stall to whinny, and looking out Ian saw that it was Dandy who was being led towards the ramp and out for exercise on the cinder yard. The big Shire paused to turn his head and whinny back to his small friend, and then Bill led him forward again. The black horse looked very full of himself this morning, walking slightly sideways at Bill's side, and shaking his big head when Bill told him to 'Steady'.

'Easy now,' Bill said to him, as they reached the ramp, and Ian turned back to his grooming as they started down into the dimness.

Ian had only run the body brush once over Magic's quarters when there was a sudden uproar from the ramp, thumps and bangs, a shout from Bill, and a final, much heavier thud. Magic flung up his head to listen, and Ian dropped his brush.

'Whatever was that?' exclaimed Angela, from the next stall.

'I don't know. I'm going to find out.' Ian was stepping over the bale.

'Wait for me.' Angela's legs were not long enough for her to step over, but by getting right down on hands and knees she could crawl underneath. Moonshine gave a friendly push as she wriggled under, and then she and Ian were hurrying down the stable towards the ramp.

There were voices coming from lower down now, out of sight round the bend of the ramp, and some heavy thumps.

'I'm going to look,' said Ian, starting carefully down the rather slippery, worn cobbles. Rather nervously, Angela followed him.

On the bend Ian stopped short, and behind him Angela gasped. Dandy had slipped on the turn, and fallen, and now he was 'cast', his head and back lower than his legs, which were pointing up the ramp. Bill was sitting on his head to prevent him from struggling, and Mr Massey and two of the stablemen were hurriedly spreading a bale of peat over the cobbles around him to make them less slippery.

'Have to turn him over,' he said, straightening up. 'He'll never make it in that position.'

'There isn't room,' objected Bill. 'He'll get jammed on his back if we try to pull him over on this bend.'

Mr Massey scratched his head, and Dandy made a heaving attempt to get his head free. Bill sat tight, soothing the horse with his hands and voice until Dandy lay still again.

'Fool horse,' Mr Massey looked down at the big black shape. 'What a place to start playing tricks.'

'What about putting some ropes round him

and pulling him down to the yard?' suggested one of the stablemen.

'There aren't enough of us,' Mr Massey looked round. 'Just three. We'll have to leave Bill at his head. We might move him, but it needs to be done slow and steady, and that means some behind to hold him back as well.'

'There's us,' said Ian, from the shadows behind Dandy. 'We could help.' Mr Massey looked up, startled.

'What are you kids doing there?' he demanded. 'Don't come any closer, I don't want you getting hurt. This is no place for you, anyway.'

'But we could help,' insisted Ian. 'We can both pull on a rope.'

'You haven't the weight,' objected Mr Massey. 'No, we can't do it that way.'

For a moment there was silence, while everyone gazed at Dandy and thought. Then, from up in the top stable, came a sudden, shrill whinny. Magic was curious, he knew that something had happened, and he sensed that it involved his friend, Dandy. Then he whinnied again, and suddenly Ian had an idea.

'The ponies!' he exclaimed. 'Magic and

Moonshine. Couldn't they help? They're pretty strong and sensible.'

'Now that's an idea, Pat,' said Bill. 'There is a lot of strength in those little fellows.'

'Have to get them down here first, though.' Mr Massey looked doubtful. 'I don't see how we'd do that, with the ramp blocked.'

'They could get by,' Ian was eager to prove that his idea could work. 'They don't need much space, and they really are sensible.'

Mr Massey made up his mind. 'All right,' he said. 'Cut round by the steps and get their harness. We'll get some ropes round this fellow, and we'll see what they can do. There's no time to waste, certainly, a cast horse can panic at any moment, and if he really does that ...' He shrugged, and the children knew that he meant Dandy could easily injure himself seriously if he was not rescued soon. They turned to hurry back up the ramp and down the stairs to the harness room for the ponies' harness.

Magic and Moonshine knew that something serious was happening. They stood quite still to have their harness on, without any of their usual playful sidling and nuzzling, and Magic stood with his ears pricked and head turned towards the ramp where he knew that Dandy had disappeared. When they were harnessed Ian took down both bales, and the ponies followed them quickly along the stable to the top of the ramp where Mr Massey was waiting for them.

'We've got some ropes round him,' he said. 'First awkward bit will be getting these two past him. Can you manage, or shall we take over?'

'I can manage,' Ian told him. 'What about you, Angie?'

'Yes, it's all right.' Angela was a bit nervous but she was not going to hand Moonshine over to Mr Massey. If Ian could help then so could she. She took a firmer hold of Moonshine's rein and followed Ian as he led Magic on to the ramp.

There was a narrow space between Dandy's head and the wall, on the steepest angle of the ramp, where it turned. Usually they led the ponies down on the other side, where the slope took a wider, shallower turn. Magic pricked his ears and whickered when he saw Dandy's great, ungainly bulk spread across the ramp, with Bill sitting on his head. Dandy's big nostrils fluttered, and he whickered back, a deep,

anxious sound. Magic replied, almost sooth-
ingly, and Ian patted him. Then, with Mr
Massey anxiously watching, he led Magic forward again. The little pony picked his way neatly
and carefully down the extreme edge of the ramp,
and it occurred to Ian that for the first time the
ponies were not a joke to Mr Massey and the
men. They were being asked to do a difficult,
responsible job, one that none of the big horses
could have attempted in the confined space,
and Ian made up his mind that they were going
to do it well.

Magic was past Dandy by now, and glancing
back Ian saw Angela leading Moonshine down.
Her hand was very tight on his rein, and her
voice as she encouraged him sounded slightly
shaky, but he knew that it was better for he and
Angela to handle the ponies rather than the
men, whom they did not know as well. Then
Moonshine was past Dandy as well, and Mr
Massey said, 'Good. Well done. Now, stop
them just there, and we'll get them hitched
up.'

There were ropes around the Shire's big body
now, and Mr Massey fastened one each to
Magic and Moonshine's breast collars. Then he

ran them round in front of the ponies' chests, and back to join the loop around Dandy. When he had finished both ponies were harnessed to the cast Shire, close together, but on separate ropes. Mr Massey checked the knots, made sure that there was plenty of peat spread on the lower part of the ramp and in the yard at the bottom, and rejoined the children.

'We're ready,' he said. 'Geoff, you and Steven get up behind him, and hold him back so he doesn't skid down too fast. Bill, keep by his head in case we have trouble. You've got the blindfold tight, have you?'

Dandy now had a scarf tied firmly over his eyes to help prevent him from struggling when Bill got off his head.

'Yes, it's tight,' Bill told Mr Massey.

Geoff and Steven had taken up their positions behind and above Dandy, the extra ropes that were fastened to him in their hands. Then Bill slowly stood up. Dandy gave one experimental heave, and then lay still.

'Right, now, start them pulling,' ordered Mr Massey. 'Slow and steady, mind.'

'Come on, Magic,' said Ian.

For a moment Magic did not move. He

turned his head to look back at Dandy, and he whickered again, long and deeply, so that his sides vibrated. It was as though he was telling the black horse that everything was all right. Then Ian urged him forward again, and Magic leaned forward smoothly into his collar. Beside him, Moonshine, encouraged by Angela, did the same, and behind them, slowly and gently, Dandy began to slide down the ramp.

'Keep it steady,' said Mr Massey, who was hovering close by in case a stronger hand was needed for the ponies. But Magic and Moonshine might have been pulling cast horses down ramps all their lives. Smoothly and steadily they moved down the ramp, pulling easily in unison, their feet sure on the peat, their heads bent forward. Behind them Dandy slid slowly, back first, round the bend and on to the last, straight slope, with Geoff and Steven holding his weight back from too fast a slide and Bill staying close to his head.

'That's fine,' said Mr Massey. 'Just keep them like that. We're almost there.'

Ian's hands were damp by now, and sweat was running down his back as he concentrated on managing the pony. Beside him, Angela's face was pale, but she was keeping a firm, sensible feel on Moonshine's bit. They were nearly at the bottom now, the greyish daylight brightening around them. Ian had time to notice with part of his mind that there were several strangers out there, watching, and then Mr Massey's 'Easy, now. Bring him down the last bit gently,' brought his full attention back to what they were doing. Suddenly Magic and Moonshine were out in the yard, still pulling steadily, and behind them the big black bulk of Dandy was pulled slowly off the last slope of the ramp on to the flat, peat-strewn yard. The ponies' part of the rescue was over.

8 · The new landlord

When the ropes were finally off Dandy, and the blindfold removed, for a moment he did not move.

'Come on then, boy,' Bill encouraged him. 'You're all right now, you can get up.'

Still Dandy did not try to pull his legs under him. Watching, the children wondered if he was hurt. Then Magic, who was watching as well, suddenly thrust his head forward and whinnied. Dandy raised his head, saw his friend watching him, and suddenly he drew his legs under him, stretched out his neck, and in one lunge he was on his feet. There was a subdued cheer from the men, and Bill began to pat Dandy, soothing the big horse. Sweat showed dark on the big body, and peat and shavings were stuck to his usually shining coat, and caught in his mane and tail. Magic was fidgeting to get closer, and Ian let him go across to nuzzle the big Shire. Dandy put his head down to the pony, and for a moment they stood quietly, nose to nose. Then Dandy took a deep, sighing breath, and Mr Massey said, 'Better take him round to the back, Bill, and lead him round until he cools off. I'll get the vet up to have a look at him.'

'That was a fine job your ponies did,' said a voice beside Ian, as Dandy was led away. He looked round to see one of the strangers he had noticed in the yard smiling down at him.

'They were good,' replied Ian. 'I knew they'd be able to do it, although I don't think Mr Massey was quite so sure.'

'Well, they certainly must have convinced him,' said the man. 'It looks to me as though they saved that horse from being seriously injured.'

Then Mr Massey came back from seeing Dandy on to the cinder yard, and joined the children and the stranger.

'Good morning Mr Champney,' he said. 'You found us having a bit of difficulty, I'm afraid.'

So this was Mr Champney, the owner of Champney's brewery, and of many of the public houses in the district. He was a big, well-dressed man with grey hair and a pleasant smile.

'Morning Massey,' he said now. 'These two little fellows saved the day, by the look of things. I was just telling this young man that they did a fine job.'

'They certainly did.' Mr Massey felt in his pocket, and immediately Magic and Moonshine's ears shot forward, their noses went up, and they began to 'ask' with their front feet. Mr Champney and his friends laughed, and came to pat the ponies while Mr Massey fed them on slices of carrot. Then Mr Champney asked how the ponies came to be at the brewery, and Mr Massey began to try to explain tactfully. There was no real reason why Mr Champney should object to the stable having an odd boarder now and then, but he felt that it should be carefully explained. But suddenly Angela interrupted. Before Mr Massey could say anything she had plunged into the full story of Uncle Arthur's new landlord, and the ponies having to be moved, and of their so far hopeless search for new, permanent stabling. Mr Champney listened in silence, his hands in the pockets of his elegant overcoat, and Ian fiddled with Magic's mane and hoped that Angela was not going to make things worse by her story. But at the end Mr Champney merely nodded.

'Your Uncle's shop is near the "Red Lion", is it?' he asked. 'Yes, I know the area. Well, your ponies are certainly very welcome to stay on here while Mr Massey has room. I wish I could say they could stay longer. I don't expect having them over here is really ideal for you, though, is it?'

'No, it's too far from the shop,' Angela told him. 'Grace has to look after it while Uncle Arthur comes over here, and then she can't give her piano lessons. And getting here in the morning makes sorting the papers a dreadful rush.'

'So I can imagine,' said Mr Champney. 'Well, I'm certainly grateful to your ponies for what they did today, and as I say they can stay here as long as there's room.'

He gave the ponies a final pat, and then Angela and Ian took them back to their stalls.

On the way Ian said, 'Whatever made you tell Mr Champney all that about them?'

'I don't know really,' Angela was surprised herself. 'It just somehow seemed a good idea. Anyway, he did say that they can stay here as long as there's room, didn't he?'

'Yes. But it hasn't really got us much further,' Ian pointed out.

Of course Uncle Arthur and Grace were very interested in the children's story of the morning's adventure.

'That'll show old Bill and the others that they aren't so useless after all,' said Uncle Arthur jubilantly. 'Good for you, Ian, for thinking of using them.'

'Was Dandy all right?' asked Grace.

'Yes. But Mr Massey said he'd better not go back upstairs until the ramp's been resurfaced,' replied Ian. 'It is a bit worn and slippery. He's changed Dandy over with one of the working horses for now.'

In spite of the praise which everyone showered on the ponies, and Mr Champney's assurance that they could stay as long as there was room, time really was getting short now. Uncle Arthur would have to decide soon about the offer from Swales and Lawrence, and only three days after Dandy's fall Mr Massey told Uncle Arthur that he had heard some news about the expected pair of new horses.

'They'll be arriving in about two weeks,' he said. 'We might still be able to find a corner for your two, but I'm afraid it wouldn't be so comfortable. We could convert a corner of the feed store for them, perhaps, or the forge.'

But Uncle Arthur thought of the time he was spending away from the shop, and the fact that he had a family to support. And he thought of Grace's cancelled piano lessons and the late morning papers.

'No,' he told Mr Massey. 'I'll have them out by then. If nothing turns up closer to my place before that they'll have to go. Can't go on like this for too long, you know.'

'I could feed them for you, if it'd help,' offered Mr Massey, but Uncle Arthur shook his head.

'It's good of you,' he said. 'But if I can't manage to look after them myself they'd be better out of my hands altogether.'

The next week was a miserable one for everyone at Uncle Arthur's. The thought of the ponies' being sold hung unhappily over them all, and even Grace could do little to cheer them up. The news spread to most of Uncle Arthur's customers, and they nearly all had something sympathetic to say when they came into the shop, but no-one could help. On Friday afternoon Angela and Ian went in through the back door while Uncle Arthur put the van away and found Grace in the living-room rather hastily taking off her coat and head-scarf.

'Mrs Randall's been minding the shop for me,' she explained, as they looked at her in surprise. Mrs Randall had helped Uncle Arthur in the shop before he married Grace, but she was usually too busy these days with another part-time job. 'I heard of somewhere that sounded possible for the ponies,' Grace went on. 'But it was hopeless. I didn't want Arthur to know, because I was afraid it might not be any good, and I didn't want to disappoint him again.'

'You don't think he will find anywhere now, do you, Grace?' asked Ian soberly.

Grace looked at them sadly. 'No,' she said. 'I'm afraid he won't. And I know that we shall miss the ponies, but Arthur will miss them much more.'

'But he can't sell them,' cried Angela. 'He can't. Oh Grace, isn't there anything we can do?'

But it did not seem that there was. Sadly, the children took off their own coats and began to set the table for tea.

Beside the ponies' going, Ian had another thing to be sad about. Without Magic and Moonshine there he did not see how he could find a reason for going on visiting the brewery stables, and that would mean the end of his newly-found satisfaction in helping with the Shires. To Ian, that was almost, though not quite, as bad as Magic and Moonshine's being sold.

That weekend there was only another week to go, and Uncle Arthur began to talk about writing to Swales and Lawrence to accept their offer for the ponies. Several times he got as far as taking the note-paper out of its drawer but each time he found an excuse to put it off.

On Sunday afternoon they all took Magic and Moonshine for a drive round the cool, grey November streets. It should have been the most exciting part of the year, with rehearsals for the pantomime starting soon, and Christmas coming, but of course it was not. Angela spent most of the drive trying not to think that it might be the last one they would ever have, and she knew that the others were feeling the same. Magic and Moonshine, however, were as gay as usual, trotting on together with a will, ears pricked, manes and tails flying, and little hooves sending echoes ringing between the tall, quiet houses.

Uncle Arthur drove them home more slowly, turning into the last street to the brewery at no more than a jog. No-one spoke until Ian and Angela were helping to unharness the ponies. Then Uncle Arthur said, 'They'll have a good home, there's that. Light work, a groom to themselves, and six weeks at grass every summer. They'll be in clover.'

'They will. A life of luxury,' agreed Grace as cheerfully as she could, and Angela hoped that she was not going to cry.

Breakfast on Monday was a silent affair. The children knew that while they were at school Uncle Arthur would write to Swales and Lawrence and the ponies would be sold. They were sitting down to scrambled eggs on toast when Uncle Arthur came in from the shop where he had been sorting the papers. He was carrying some letters that the postman had just left, and he dropped them on the table while Grace brought in the teapot.

'Anything interesting?' she asked, trying to sound as usual.

'The electricity bill,' replied Uncle Arthur dismally. 'And some sort of circular. I don't know what the other is, probably a letter from a cross customer.'

'Hadn't you better open it?' asked Grace, as he picked up his knife and fork.

'I suppose so.' Uncle Arthur was not very interested in his breakfast anyway. He picked up the envelope and tore it open, and for a moment no-one spoke. Then Grace said sharply, 'Do you feel all right, Arthur?' and Ian and Angela looked up. Uncle Arthur certainly looked very peculiar. His face had gone white, and was now starting to go scarlet instead, and his hands were shaking so much that the sheet of notepaper he was holding rustled.

'Arthur,' said Grace again, and this time Uncle Arthur looked up.

'Here,' he said. 'You read it. Tell me I'm not dreaming.'

Grace took the letter from him, and as she read she too began to look excited.

'Oh, what is it? Please tell us.' Angela could not bear it any longer.

'It's from Mr Champney, the owner of the brewery,' replied Grace, in a tight, excited sort of voice. 'He, or rather the brewery company, have bought all this property. They're going to develop "The Red Lion" and the old wine shop next door into one of their new pubs, with a grill-room for people to eat in. And . . . and he says that as far as he's concerned it will be quite all right for us to have the ponies in the yard again. He says he's glad to have the opportunity to thank them in some way for saving Dandy.'

'You mean, it's all right?' Ian felt dazed. 'They can come back?'

'Then they needn't be sold?' Angela felt her face going scarlet with excitement. 'They really needn't?'

'No, they really needn't,' Grace was looking across the table at Uncle Arthur. 'You aren't dreaming Arthur.'

'Hurrah,' Ian was on his feet, his breakfast forgotten, and Angela was hugging first Grace and then Uncle Arthur. And Uncle Arthur's face was one enormous, beaming smile.

'Come on,' he said, leaping to his feet. 'Let's go and tell them. They know something's been up, they've probably been worrying themselves.'

'Arthur, you haven't eaten your breakfast,' protested Grace.

'The kids have. I can have something later.' Uncle Arthur swung round the table, seized Grace, and gave her a smacking kiss. 'See you later, love. Come on, you two, let's get down there.'

Ian and Angela grabbed their coats and rushed after him, leaving Grace on the kitchen steps laughing and waving and shaking her head.

'I'll get the stable swept out if I have time,' she called, and Uncle Arthur paused to wave and grin at her from the yard gate.

They brought Magic and Moonshine home that afternoon, after school. All the men at the brewery came out to wave them off, and Magic and Moonshine gave a last performance of their tricks for rewards of carrots and sugar from everyone.

'We shall miss them,' said Mr Massey. 'But I'm taking my wife and kids along to Wembley to see them in "Cinderella". Come round and see us some time, won't you? And if you want to go on giving us a hand with the big fellows, Ian, you'll be welcome any time.'

'Thank you,' said Ian, and beamed at Mr Massey with real gratitude. So he wouldn't lose his Shires after all. From inside the stable Dandy, hearing the disturbance outside, whinnied, and Magic whinnied back. Mr Massey smiled.

'There's another who'll miss them,' he said. 'But he'll be going in harness soon, and he'll find himself another pal then. But it's been a real experience for us all, knowing these two.'

Most of Uncle Arthur's neighbours had come out to see Magic and Moonshine return home. Someone had even gone as far as to hang a strip of bunting across the end of the cinder path, and the ponies came down the ramp to a royal welcome. All the local children had brought them 'welcome home' gifts of food, and Magic and Moonshine nodded and bowed and kissed and shook hands until they were dizzy. Uncle Arthur was in the middle of it all, red-faced and

beaming, and Partner watched from a grandstand seat on the wall.

But at last the ponies were through the gate
and inside their own shed, and the neighbours
had drifted away. Standing in deep, clean
straw, with large feeds and crammed hay nets
in front of them, the ponies seemed to look
around and take deep, satisfied breaths. They
had been happy enough at Champney's, but it
was not their own place. This was, and their
contented expressions as they began to eat said
that they were glad to be back.

'Here comes Partner,' said Grace, and the
big ginger cat stalked in through the door,

paused, and then leaped lightly up on to the partition, and into his usual place on Magic's back.

'He's missed that,' said Grace. 'He's certainly glad to see them back.'

'He isn't the only one,' Uncle Arthur put his arm round her. 'Do you know, I really thought I was going to have to sell them. My goodness, I'd have missed them.'

'So would we all,' replied Grace, hugging him. 'Now, come on. Tea's waiting.'

She led the way out into the yard, where Uncle Arthur closed the shed door on the contented munching. And as he followed the others across the yard Ian knew that the family was complete again, and that now, like the others, he really was a part of it.

A. D. LANGHOLM

The Clover Club Books

Exciting stories of mystery and adventure, guaranteed to keep you guessing all the time, involving four children – Sarah, Tom, Graham and Rodge – who form themselves into a secret club.

The Clover Club and The House of Mystery

The children investigate a ghostly figure who visits a decaying house inhabited by an elderly lady. It is Sarah's idea to pursue the mystery of Miss Maybury's house – but she needs help and first has to persuade the boys to let her become a member of the Clover Club.

The Clover Club and the Adventure That Fell Out of the Sky

The Club exists to have adventures – but if none just happen, you must invent them. So the boys decide to track Herr Becker, a harmless German tourist, and pretend he's a wartime spy. Following him along the country lanes, the four children soon discover he isn't just a tourist after all ...

Each illustrated by Reginald Gray

MARY O'HARA

My Friend Flicka

Ken McLaughlin loves his life on the ranch in Wyoming but the thing he dreams about most of all is having a colt of his very own. Then one day, whilst riding the range, his dreams come true – he sees the filly he has always wanted – his Flicka.

Thunderhead

Following on from *My Friend Flicka*, *Thunderhead* continues the story of the McLaughlin family and their horses at the Goose Bar Ranch. Ken dreams of turning Flicka's colt, Thunderhead, into an unbeatable racehorse. A moving and exciting story of a boy and a colt growing up together.

Green Grass of Wyoming

The last of the three Flicka books, in which the saga of the Goose Bar Ranch reaches its peak. The McLaughlins live through a series of dramatic incidents, and Ken begins to grow up fast. Then Thunderhead, the superb stallion, roams far away into the Wyoming hills and he is the only one in the end who can help Ken prove himself to the world.

These and other Magnet Books are available at your bookshop or newsagent. In case of difficulties, orders may be sent to:

Magnet Books
Cash Sales Department
PO Box 11
Falmouth
Cornwall TR10 9EN
England

Please send cheque or postal order, no currency, for purchase price quoted and allow the following for postage and packing:

U.K. CUSTOMERS
40p for the first book, plus 18p for the second book and 13p for each additional book ordered, to a maximum charge of £1.49p.

B.F.P.O. & EIRE
40p for the first book, plus 18p for the second book and 13p per copy for the next 7 books, thereafter 7p per book.

OVERSEAS CUSTOMERS
60p for the first book, plus 18p per copy for each additional book.

While every effort is made to keep prices low, it is sometimes necessary to increase prices at short notice. Magnet Books reserve the right to show new retail prices on covers which may differ from those previously advertised in the text or elsewhere.